Biography Today

Profiles of People of Interest to Young Readers

Sports

Volume 12

Cherie D. Abbey
Managing Editor

Kevin Hillstrom
Editor

615 Griswold Street • Detroit, Michigan 48226

Omnigraphics, Inc.

Cherie D. Abbey, *Managing Editor*
Kevin Hillstrom, *Editor*

Laurie Hillstrom, *Sketch Writer*

Allison A. Beckett, Mary Butler, and Linda Strand, *Research Staff*

* * *

Peter E. Ruffner, *Publisher*
Frederick G. Ruffner, Jr., *Chairman*
Matthew P. Barbour, *Senior Vice President*
Kay Gill, *Vice President — Directories*

* * *

Liz Barbour, *Permissions Associate*
Dave Bianco, *Marketing Director*
Leif A. Gruenberg, *Development Manager*
Kevin Hayes, *Operations Manager*
Barry Puckett, *Librarian*

Cherry Stockdale, *Permissions Assistant*
Shirley Amore, Don Brown, Margaret M. Geist, Kevin Glover,
Martha Johns, and Kirk Kauffman, *Contributing Staff*

Copyright © 2004 Omnigraphics, Inc.
ISBN 0-7808-0714-6

The information in this publication was compiled from the sources cited and from other sources considered reliable. While every possible effort has been made to ensure reliability, the publisher will not assume liability for damages caused by inaccuracies in the data, and makes no warranty, express or implied, on the accuracy of the information contained herein.

This book is printed on acid-free paper meeting the ANSI Z39.48 Standard. The infinity symbol that appears above indicates that the paper in this book meets that standard.

Printed in the United States

Contents

3

Preface

Welcome to the 12th volume of the **Biography Today Sports** series. We are publishing this series in response to suggestions from our readers, who want more coverage of more people in *Biography Today*. Several volumes, covering **Artists, Authors, Performing Artists, Scientists and Inventors, Sports Figures, and World Leaders,** have appeared thus far in the Subject Series. Each of these hardcover volumes is 200 pages in length and covers approximately 10 individuals of interest to readers ages 9 and above. The length and format of the entries are like those found in the regular issues of *Biography Today*, but there is **no duplication** between the regular series and the special subject volumes.

The Plan of the Work

As with the regular issues of *Biography Today*, this special subject volume on **Sports** was especially created to appeal to young readers in a format they can enjoy reading and readily understand. Each volume contains alphabetically arranged sketches. Each entry provides at least one picture of the individual profiled, and bold-faced rubrics lead the reader to information on birth, youth, early memories, education, first jobs, marriage and family, career highlights, memorable experiences, hobbies, and honors and awards. Each of the entries ends with a list of easily accessible sources designed to lead the student to further reading on the individual and a current address. Obituary entries are also included, written to provide a perspective on the individual's entire career. Obituaries are clearly marked in both the table of contents and at the beginning of the entry.

Biographies are prepared by Omnigraphics editors after extensive research, utilizing the most current materials available. Those sources that are generally available to students appear in the list of further reading at the end of the sketch.

Indexes

A new index now appears in all *Biography Today* publications. In an effort to make the index easier to use, we have combined the **Name** and **General Index** into one, called the **Cumulative Index**. This new index contains the names of all individuals who have appeared in *Biography Today* since the series began. The names appear in bold faced type, followed by the issue in which they appeared. The Cumulative Index also contains the occupations, nationalities, and ethnic and minority origins of individuals profiled. The Cumulative Index is cumulative, including references to all individuals who have appeared in the *Biography Today* General Series and the *Biography Today* Special Subject volumes since the series began in 1992.

The Birthday Index and Places of Birth Index will continue to appear in all Special Subject volumes.

Our Advisors

This series was reviewed by an Advisory Board comprised of librarians, children's literature specialists, and reading instructors to ensure that the concept of this publication — to provide a readable and accessible biographical magazine for young readers — was on target. They evaluated the title as it developed, and their suggestions have proved invaluable. Any errors, however, are ours alone. We'd like to list the Advisory Board members, and to thank them for their efforts.

Our Advisory Board stressed to us that we should not shy away from controversial or unconventional people in our profiles, and we have tried to follow their advice. The Advisory Board also mentioned that the sketches might be useful in reluctant reader and adult literacy programs, and we would value any comments librarians might have about the suitability of our magazine for those purposes.

Your Comments Are Welcome

Our goal is to be accurate and up-to-date, to give young readers information they can learn from and enjoy. Now we want to know what you think. Take a look at this issue of *Biography Today*, on approval. Write or call me with your comments. We want to provide an excellent source of biographical information for young people. Let us know how you think we're doing.

Cherie Abbey
Managing Editor, *Biography Today*
Omnigraphics, Inc.
615 Griswold Street
Detroit, MI 48226

editor@biographytoday.com
www.biographytoday.com

Freddy Adu 1989-

Ghana-Born American Professional Soccer Player
with D.C. United
Youngest Person to Play in a Major American
Professional Sports League

BIRTH

Fredua Adu (pronounced *ah-DOO*), known as Freddy, was born
on June 2, 1989, in Tema, Ghana. Ghana is a country in West
Africa, and Tema is a bustling port city on the Gulf of Guinea.
Freddy's parents, Maxwell and Emelia Adu, operated a department store there. Freddy has a younger brother who is also

named Fredua (giving two children the same first name is a common custom in Ghanian families), but he is known by the nickname Fro. The Adu family moved to the United States in 1997, when Freddy was eight years old. Maxwell Adu left the family shortly after its arrival, and Freddy and Fro have not seen their father since. The boys and their mother became naturalized American citizens in February 2003.

YOUTH

Freddy has fond memories of his boyhood in Ghana. Ghana is one of the more politically and economically stable countries in West Africa, and his family enjoyed a simple but comfortable life there. Soccer is a national passion in Ghana, as it is in much of Europe and South America. "In Ghana, soccer is what you play," Freddy explained. "Barefoot, in the streets." Freddy had an uncle in the United States who sent him his first soccer ball when he was about two years old. "I remember the first time Freddy held a soccer ball," his mother related. "His eyes lit up and he got a big smile. He knew right away that there was something special about it." From that time on, Freddy never wanted to be separated from his favorite toy. "My mom said that when she'd take the ball away, I'd start crying," he noted.

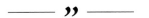

> "I remember the first time Freddy held a soccer ball," Adu's mother related. "His eyes lit up and he got a big smile. He knew right away that there was something special about it."

Over the next several years, Freddy honed his skills by playing soccer in the streets of Tema against boys who were much older and bigger than him. "Whenever we came back from school we would just take a soccer ball and go outside and there would be 20 guys out there waiting to play," he recalled. "I was the supplier of balls in the neighborhood. We'd just go out there and play nonstop until it got dark. We'd play every day. We didn't go a day without playing." In all this time, Freddy never played on an organized team or received any formal coaching. Instead, he and his friends invented their own moves and practice methods. "We'd see a game on TV, and we'd try to duplicate the skills of what the top players in the world did," he said. "Sometimes it worked, sometimes it didn't."

In 1997 Freddy's family won a U.S. State Department lottery and received a green card allowing them to immigrate to America. His parents decided to move to the United States in order to give their sons the best possible educational opportunities. "My family thought it would be good for us to go to school in the U.S.," Freddy recalled. "We weren't even thinking about soccer." So, at the age of eight, Freddy suddenly found himself in the unfamiliar environment of Potomac, Maryland, a suburb of Washington, D.C.

Within a year of Freddy's arrival in the United States, his father left the family. His absence forced Adu's mother to work 70 hours per week in two different jobs in order to support her sons. Each day Emelia would send the boys off to school and go to work at McDonald's. After coming home to prepare their dinner, she went to work at her other job cleaning a nearby office building. She would return home long after the boys were asleep.

As Freddy struggled to adjust to a new culture and climate, the thing he missed most was soccer. "When I came here, I wouldn't see anybody playing in the streets," he recalled. "It was cold, snow everywhere, and people told me that most American kids have other activities." He tried playing basketball for a while, but found that he did not enjoy it nearly as much as soccer.

One day, Freddy started playing pick-up soccer with some of his fourth-grade classmates. One of his friends was so dazzled by his footwork and ballhandling skills that he invited Freddy to try out for his club soccer team. His talents soon impressed everyone in the league. After just a few games, Freddy was recruited to join an elite Under-14 (U-14) travel team, the Potomac Cougars. "He had all the instinctive skills to play soccer, as if they had been bestowed upon him," said Cougars Coach Arnold Tarzy, who became a close friend and adviser to the Adu family. "It was beyond imagining."

Over the next few years, Freddy's reputation as a rising soccer star spread far and wide. In both 1999 and 2000 he helped the U.S. Olympic Development Program win a major youth tournament in Italy against the development squads of several major European professional soccer clubs. Although Freddy was the youngest player in the tournament, he was selected as its most valuable player both years. His performance in Italy attracted attention from the European clubs. When he was just ten years old, one of the top Italian professional teams, Inter Milan, offered him a $750,000 contract to join its youth program. His mother rejected the offer, however, because she felt Freddy was not ready. "Our family was just kind of barely well off," he remembered. "It had to be tough for her not to take that amount of money." In 2001 Freddy led the Potomac Cougars to the U-14 National Championship.

EDUCATION

After moving to the United States, Adu completed the fourth and fifth grades in the public schools in Potomac, Maryland. In sixth grade he received a scholarship based on financial need to enroll at The Heights, a private school in Potomac. Thanks to his excellent grades, he skipped seventh grade and was promoted to eighth grade the following year. As a high school freshman at The Heights in 2001, Adu scored 25 goals and had 12 assists in 16 games to lead his team to the Maryland state independent high school soccer championship. He was also named a high-school all-American as a freshman. "Sometimes a huge crowd would turn up just to see me play," he recalled. "It was like I was supposed to be Superman."

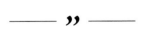

> "Sometimes a huge crowd would turn up just to see me play," said Adu. "It was like I was supposed to be Superman."

In the middle of his freshman year of high school, Adu decided to join the U.S. Soccer Federation's residency program. He made the decision after working out with the team several times, visiting the school with his family, and talking extensively with the coaches. This program allowed him to live, train, and compete with the U.S. National Under-17 soccer team, which featured the top 30 young players in the country. It also enabled him to complete his high school education at an accelerated pace at the Edison Learning Center at IMG Academy in Bradenton, Florida. Along with his teammates, Adu underwent several hours of intensive instruction each morning, followed by an afternoon of soccer practice. He also traveled to tournaments in Brazil, France, and other countries.

When Adu entered the residency program in January 2002 at the age of 12, he became the youngest player ever to train with the U-17 team. He felt that joining the national team program was a better choice for his long-term future than continuing to play with local school and club teams in Maryland or signing a six-figure contract to play junior soccer for a European professional team. For one thing, the program guaranteed that he would receive a high school diploma. "My mom won't let me go anywhere until I graduate," Adu noted.

Adu continued to impress people with his performance on the soccer field during his years with the U-17 team. He also did extremely well in the classroom, earning straight-As and completing his high school equivalency in May 2004, shortly before his 15th birthday.

Adu and his mother, Emelia, at a 2003 press conference announcing his decision to play Major League Soccer (MLS).

CAREER HIGHLIGHTS

The U.S. National Under-17 Team

Adu began training with the U.S. National Under-17 team in January 2002, when he joined the U.S. Soccer Federation's residency program. He played in only 35 of the squad's 66 matches that season, but he still ranked second on the team with 22 goals and tied for the team lead with 11 assists. His production included two goals in an exhibition match against the Chicago Fire, an American professional team from Major League Soccer (MLS). Even some of Adu's teammates had trouble believing that a 12-year-old could possess such amazing skills. "I said, 'There's no way, this is just hype.' I saw this little kid walking up," 17-year-old Jamie Watson re-

13

called of meeting Adu for the first time. "After the first practice, I left with my jaw hanging. Now I joke about it at practice: 'Do something I've never seen before,' and he does something physically impossible."

During the 2003 season, Adu led the U.S. team in goals (23) and assists (14) leading up to the U-17 World Championships in Finland. He impressed observers around the world by scoring a hat trick (three goals) against South Korea in the American team's first match of the World Championships. Later in the tournament, Adu overcame a series of fouls to score the game-winning goal in the final minutes of play in a match against Sierra Leone. "You're getting hit the whole game, not getting any calls, and the opposing team is talking all this trash," he recalled. "The only way to shut them up is to get a goal. It just breaks them." Adu's goal helped the U.S. team advance to the quarter-finals of the tournament, where they were knocked out. A few months later, Adu posted another hat trick against Poland at a high-profile tournament in France.

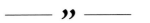

"You're getting hit the whole game, not getting any calls, and the opposing team is talking all this trash," Adu recalled. "The only way to shut them up is to get a goal. It just breaks them."

In May 2003, Adu signed a $1 million endorsement deal with Nike, the sporting goods manufacturer. As the 2003 season progressed, it became clear that the young man had some important decisions to make regarding his future. He continued to receive lucrative offers from European professional soccer clubs. Although he hoped to play in Europe eventually, Adu knew that FIFA — soccer's international governing body — did not allow young players to join the elite teams until they turned 18. Therefore, he would be forced to play on a developmental squad for several years if he signed with a European team. "I don't want to get stuck in some youth system where my development hits a brick wall," he noted. "I love soccer so much, I want to play." Adu also considered playing college soccer in the United States, but he knew that the level of competition would not be as strong as it was at the professional level.

Adu ultimately decided to sign a contract to play in the American professional soccer league, Major League Soccer (MLS). In his view, this option offered a number of advantages: it allowed him to remain at home with his family, see immediate playing time against professional competition, and put money away for his education. "We wanted to allow Freddy to pursue his dreams and develop his God-given talents," his mother explained. "As he makes this next step at the age of 14, it was best for Freddy to stay in America and sign with MLS." "It just gives me a chance to be me, really, be with my family and just be a normal kid," Adu added. "Everyone is like, 'Oh, could you have signed with European teams?' I could have, but I decided not to because I have a long way to go, and I want to mature and be at home for a little bit. And when the right time comes, I get the opportunity to go."

When Adu's signing was announced in November 2003, journalists and soccer officials described him as a potential savior of MLS and American soccer. MLS came into existence in 1996, but it never gained much attention from the public or the media. The ten teams in the league drew an average of 15,000 fans per match, but MLS still struggled financially, losing an estimated $100 million over the years. Many people hoped that Adu would bring much-needed fans and revenue to the league. "This is the biggest signing in the history of our league," said MLS Commissioner Don Garber. "Adu is widely considered the best young soccer player in the world and we believe that playing in his home country in MLS will further develop him as a player and most importantly as a person. . . . This is a great day not just for MLS, but for soccer in America."

Major League Soccer — D.C. United

In early 2004 Adu was officially assigned to D.C. United, the MLS team closest to his home in Maryland. He signed a four-year contract worth an estimated $500,000 per season. This yearly salary made the 14-year-old Adu the highest-paid player in MLS. His pay was even higher than that of league superstars who were 10-15 years older than him.

D.C. United had been one of the best teams in the early years of the league, winning three MLS championships in its first four seasons. But then the team fell on hard times, missing the playoffs the next three years before barely sneaking in again in 2003. As the 2004 season approached, Adu expressed his intention to turn the team around. "Hopefully, I can do something to help the team get back to its winning ways," he stated. "The first few years, D.C. was the team to beat. I still think that we have the talent and the team to win."

Adu made his professional debut on April 3, 2004, in a D.C. United home game against the San Jose Earthquakes. He thus became the youngest person in over 100 years to play in a major American professional sports league. (The youngest ever was Fred Chapman, who pitched a few innings for the Philadelphia Athletics in 1887 at age 14.) "If you're good enough,

Adu (left) prepares to strike the ball on goal in a 2004 contest against the Los Angeles Galaxy.

you're old enough," Adu stated. "If you feel like you're ready to go, hey, give it a shot." Unfortunately, Adu appeared very nervous when he entered the game as a late substitution, and he did not contribute to D.C. United's 2-1 victory. "I wasn't nervous all week before the season started," he said. "But when I stepped out there on the field, that was the worst I've felt, I think, in my whole life."

Adu looked much more confident in his next game. He scored his first professional goal on April 17, in only his third game—a 3-2 loss to the MetroStars. By the time D.C. United played its fifth game of the season, Adu had broken into the team's starting lineup. Although he felt confident that he could contribute to his team's success, Adu also realized that he had a lot to learn. "I think I could be an impact player this season," he stated. "But I'm not always going to have the greatest game of my life. There's going to be games when I absolutely suck. That happens to everybody. So it'll be up to me to regroup and try to find a way to bounce back." Adu also recognized that being the league's highest-paid player might lead opponents to key on him. "I'm going to have a big X on my back now, because some of these guys have been in the league a long time, and here comes this 14-year-old kid making this amount of money," he noted. "But I didn't think it was going to be easy when I made this decision, and I'm ready for it."

Meanwhile, Adu's presence on the field had an immediate effect on Major League Soccer's financial fortunes. D.C. United's attendance increased by 7,000 fans per game — both at home and on the road — and the team also generated record TV ratings for MLS. Merchandise sales increased as well, with Adu's number 11 jersey an especially popular item. "It's been great even though I haven't been playing as well and as much as I would have liked to, but I'm a rookie and I have to pay my dues," he said. "I have to earn my place and I'm going to keep working hard."

Comparisons to the Sport's Greats

Adu's rapid ascent to the top ranks of his sport triggers constant comparisons between him and the legendary Brazilian soccer star Pele. Arguably the best soccer player in history, Pele scored six goals to lead Brazil to the World Cup title in 1956, when he was just 17 years old. (Held every four years, the World Cup tournament features the best soccer teams from each continent.) Pele helped Brazil claim two more championships, in 1962 and 1970, to become the only player ever to win three World Cups.

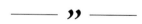

"I'm a rookie and I have to pay my dues," Adu said. "I have to earn my place and I'm going to keep working hard."

Adu resembles Pele physically — with a small build, incredible foot speed, and a low center of gravity — as well as in his graceful style of play. "He's blessed with breakneck speed, amazing acceleration, the field vision of an NFL quarterback, and deceptive strength for a 5-foot-7, 140-pounder," wrote Mark Starr in *Newsweek*. "And he possesses that critical ability to keep the ball on his foot, even under intense pressure, as if it were dangling from a string." In addition to his physical skills, many observers also feel that Adu possesses some indefinable quality that makes him better than other players. "It's more than just his talent level; there's something else about him," said John Trask, an assistant coach for D.C. United. "That's what they said about Pele. There might have been a few players at his level, but he had that something else. Freddy has that."

Adu (center) fends off an opponent as he brings the ball downfield.

An added benefit to playing for MLS is that Adu ia available to the U.S. national team for future tournaments, including the 2006 World Cup. The American men's soccer team has long received little respect in international competition. It finished last in the 1998 World Cup tournament, and few American players have made an impact in the elite European leagues. Since the turn of the century, however, a number of young stars have emerged to raise the profile of American soccer. The U.S. men's squad impressed many people by making it to the quarterfinals of the 2002 World Cup tournament, and some observers believe that as Adu further develops his skills, he will be able to help lift the U.S. team to new heights.

Adu admits that one of his biggest goals is to help win a World Cup title for the United States in 2006. "I see myself in a World Cup final for the U.S.A., playing against a top-notch team everyone picks to win . . . and we just come out and blast them," he stated. "One day when I'm holding that trophy, someone's gonna take a picture. Oh, man. That is going to be huge." In June 2004 Adu was named to the U.S. National Under-20 team, meaning that he will have the opportunity to practice and play international tournaments with the squad during the MLS off-season.

Dealing with Stardom

Adu has already received star treatment in the media. He has been profiled in feature articles in *Sports Illustrated, Vanity Fair, Newsweek,* and *USA Today.* He has demonstrated tricks with a soccer ball on "Late Night with David Letterman" and appeared in a soft-drink commercial with Pele. He cannot go out in public without being mobbed by fans, some of whom try to rip off his clothes. "It's been pretty hard, I guess, but I have fun with it," he noted. "Sometimes you want to have fun with your friends and stuff, but you go out, people recognize you and just swarm you, and you've got to start to give autographs."

Some critics have expressed concern about Adu's emotional development, saying that 14 is too young to be the face of American soccer. They worry that he will experience burnout and argue that he should have more time to enjoy a normal childhood. But others marvel at Adu's maturity and claim that he seems well-equipped to handle the spotlight. "Being a boy soccer god is a sketchy job," Rick Reilly wrote in *Sports Illustrated.* "Diego Maradona burst on the world at 15, and now he's fat and living in Cuba, where he went to treat his drug dependency. Then again, Pele was a World Cup star at 17 and is still the elegant face of his sport. This kid can handle it. . . . At 14 Freddy Adu might finally be the one to make this country fall in love with soccer."

Adu recognizes the potential drawbacks of his early fame. "A lot of people have been hyped up to be great but just disappeared," he acknowledged. "I promised myself I wouldn't be one of them." He insists that his overwhelming love of soccer will see him through. "I love having the ball at my feet and running at the defender one-on-one," he stated. "That's when I'm at my best, when I can pull some weird move and get by him and everyone goes, *Ohhhh. I love* that."

Adu was selected to participate in the MLS All-Star Game in his rookie season.

HOME AND FAMILY

Adu is single and lives at home with his mother and younger brother. He often expresses his gratitude to his mother for working so hard to provide him and his brother with opportunities. "She is so strong. Whenever there seemed like there was no way out of a situation or a jam, she always came through for my little brother and me," he stated. "So when I play now I play for her and make her happy."

Upon signing his MLS contract, Adu bought his mother a new Lexus and built a new house for the family in suburban Rockville, Maryland. The house features a huge kitchen, where his mother can indulge her love of cooking, and a basement recreation room for Freddy and Fro to enjoy. "That's the coolest part," Adu noted. "I can hang out with my friends, play pool, listen to music, and dance. It's going to be awesome, man."

Adu insisted that his mother quit working once he signed his contract. "I'm just happy to pay her back for all the things she's done for us," he explained. "All I have to do now is play the sport I love and everything will take care of itself. To see my mom just relaxing and enjoying life a little bit more makes it all worth it." Now Emelia's job consists of driving Freddy to soccer practice — at least until he is old enough to get a driver's license.

HOBBIES AND OTHER INTERESTS

In his spare time, Adu enjoys listening to hip-hop music, playing video games, watching movies, and hitting golf balls. He claims that his life is quite "normal." "Always smiling, playing video games, talking trash back and forth with my friends," he said. "There are more important things in life than soccer." Adu's favorite movies are the *Lord of the Rings* trilogy, and his favorite food is jollof rice. "It's an African stew my mom makes for me. She makes it a special way and puts the rice in so it cooks with the stew," he explained. "It's very good."

HONORS AND AWARDS

High School Soccer All-American: 2001

FURTHER READING

Periodicals

Boys' Life, Apr. 2004, p.10
Chicago Tribune, May 30, 2004, Sports, p.10

Interview, Apr. 2004, p.88
Newsday, Nov. 20, 2003, p.A74
Newsweek, Dec. 30, 2002, p.70
St. Petersburg Times, Sep. 21, 2003, p.C1
Sports Illustrated, Mar. 3, 2003, p.41; Aug. 25, 2003, p.17; Mar. 29, 2004, p.58
Sports Illustrated for Kids, Mar. 2002, p.54; July 2004, p.22
Tampa Tribune, Feb. 19, 2004, Sports, p.1
USA Today, Apr. 1, 2004, p.C1; June 9, 2004, p.C8
Washington Post, Jan. 23, 2003, p.C13; Nov. 19, 2003, p.A1; May 21, 2004, p.D3

Online Articles

http://www.soccerphile.com
  (*Soccerphile.com,* "Football Commentary: Freddy Adu," Apr. 3, 2002)
http://www.cbsnews.com/stories
  (*CBS News,* "Freddy Adu Says Hello," Nov. 20, 2003; "Freddy Adu: Just Going Out to Play," Mar. 28, 2004)
http://www.denverpost.com
  (*Denver Post,* "Freddy Adu," Jan. 11, 2004)

Online Databases

Biography Resource Center Online, 2004

ADDRESS

Freddy Adu
DC United
RFK Stadium
2400 East Capitol St. NE
Washington, D.C. 20003

WORLD WIDE WEB SITES

http://www.ussoccer.com
http://dcunited.mlsnet.com
http://www.nike.com/nikesoccer/adu

Tina Basich 1969-

American Professional Snowboarder
Winner of the Women's Big Air Gold Medal at the
1998 Winter X Games

BIRTH

Tina Basich was born on June 29, 1969, in Fair Oaks, a suburb
of Sacramento in northern California. Her father worked as a
house painter, and her mother was an artist and homemaker.
She has a younger brother, Michael, who also became a professional snowboarder.

YOUTH

Growing up, Tina was an athletic girl who enjoyed playing with her brother and other neighborhood boys. She particularly liked riding BMX bikes, skateboarding, and building forts in the backyard of her family's home. "We had about ten different tree forts in our yard, with one in almost every tree," she remembered. "We had rope swings and zip lines connecting them like a maze." Tina also took gymnastics lessons from an early age and showed some promise as a young gymnast. "My gymnastics coaches wanted to start training me for the Olympics when I was eight years old because they 'saw talent,' but I couldn't handle the pressure," she admitted. "I'd get so nervous, I'd pee in my leotard before my floor routine and run off to the bathroom, refusing to come out until my mom came and picked me up." Although her gymnastics career never took off, Tina later found the training valuable when she began performing tricks on her snowboard.

Tina's childhood changed dramatically when she was 13 and her younger brother had a severe epileptic seizure. (Epilepsy is a disorder in which nerve cells in the brain signal incorrectly, causing symptoms ranging from strange sensations to uncontrollable muscle spasms to loss of consciousness.) Michael Basich took medication to control the physical effects of his epilepsy, but he also suffered emotional and behavioral effects. He withdrew from his family, for example, and eventually lost his ability to speak.

For the next three years, Tina and her parents devoted themselves to helping Michael recover. They purchased a vacant lot in Fair Oaks and all worked together to help build a new house. While their home was under construction, they lived together in a teepee in the yard for more than six months. "You'd hear people talking about us in the grocery lines," Tina related. The family's efforts paid off, as Michael eventually regained his speech and returned to school. The whole experience had a lasting effect on Tina. "Forming that bond with my family and my brother gave me an unbelievable appreciation for life, which I think made me into the person that I am," she noted.

Discovering the Thrill of Snowboarding

In 1985 — when she was 16 years old and a sophomore in high school — Tina discovered the sport of snowboarding. Snowboarding originated in the 1960s, when adventurous young people tried sliding down snow-covered hills on surfboards or on two skis bolted together. For many years, snowboarding was considered an "outlaw" sport and was not allowed at most ski resorts. But as the equipment improved and more trend-setting youngsters took up the sport, it rapidly gained in popularity and acceptance.

On a family vacation to Lake Tahoe, Tina's mother saw a snowboard in a ski shop and recommended that Tina and Michael try it. Avid skateboarders, the siblings rented snowboards the following day and immediately fell in love with the new sport. They knew that many ski resorts forbade snowboarding on their slopes at the time, but Tina and Michael did not care. In fact, Tina enjoyed her early snowboarding experiences so much that she used her Christmas money and all of her savings to purchase her own board, a Burton Elite 140.

From the beginning, Basich was one of only a few girls involved in the fledgling sport. "We were the misfits of the misfits—the girlfriends of the rebel skateboarder guys, the anti-cheerleaders," she admitted in her auto-biography, *Pretty Good for a Girl.* "We wanted to fit in, but we didn't. Snowboarding to us was a savior. It was wholly original and something all our own. There were no role models. We made things up as we went along—stickering our boards like our school notebooks, duct-taping our equipment, cutting plastic straps to make bindings smaller around our feet, testing new tricks. The addiction was instant the first time we figured out how to link turns down a hill."

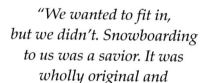

"We wanted to fit in, but we didn't. Snowboarding to us was a savior. It was wholly original and something all our own."

Basich and her fellow snowboarders even took a certain pleasure in pursuing their interest despite the disapproval of the skiing establishment. "We had to hike up the mountains next to the resorts," Tina recalled. "We were not taken well by the skiers. They thought of us as the misfit skater kids who were in the way, cutting people off."

Like most other early snowboarders, Tina created her own clothing and equipment and built her own obstacles and jumps. "Back then, if you saw someone with a snowboard, you instantly went over to them and found out what gear they had and how they modified it," she remembered. "We dug out halfpipes with shovels and the walls were maybe three feet high."

Tina's skills improved quickly, and she soon began entering snowboarding contests. As she improved, she often heard fellow snowboarders comment that she was "pretty good for a girl.""At first I took it as a compliment,"she recalled, "then I figured they were putting me aside. That's part of what motivated me to get better. I wanted to get better than the guys."

Over the next few years, Tina entered larger and more prestigious contests and began to attract the attention of sponsors. Snowboarding gradually became the main focus of her life. "Finding something that I was good at was really important, especially at this age," she noted. "It gave me something new to focus on and it was exactly what I was made for. Even though I'd been involved in team sports my whole life and learned a lot from them, snowboarding was new and exciting. I loved that."

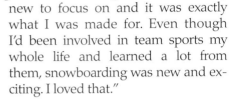

"Finding something that I was good at was really important, especially at this age," Basich noted. "It gave me something new to focus on and it was exactly what I was made for. Even though I'd been involved in team sports my whole life and learned a lot from them, snowboarding was new and exciting."

EDUCATION

Basich started out in public school, but her mother withdrew her in the middle of first grade. After overhearing a teacher criticize one of Tina's drawings, her mother grew concerned that the elementary school did not place enough emphasis on creativity. Tina repeated first grade the following year at Waldorf School — a private, arts-oriented academy in Sacramento — and remained there until ninth grade. "It was an alternative school based around the arts, music, and creative thinking," she explained. "I claim it's not a hippie school, but we did have gardening, woodworking, and beeswax classes. Our teachers told us endless stories about fairies and gnomes and I really believed in them. My artwork to this day is inspired by those fairy tales."

After leaving Waldorf, Basich moved to a large public high school in Fair Oaks. "Del Campo High School had 1,400 kids," she recalled. "I was overwhelmed to say the least. I made new friends, but didn't fit into any one group and kind of drifted between different cliques. My main niche was with a couple of skateboarders who were the only ones in my school."

Basich ran track and also participated in swimming and diving in high school. Her early involvement in snowboarding also helped her gain some recognition from her fellow students. "The first publication to run a picture

Basich has been widely saluted as a pioneer in the sport of women's snowboarding.

and story about me snowboarding was my high school paper, the *Del Campo Roar*," she remembered. "I was getting recognized for doing this cool new sport. I was the snowboarder girl."

Upon graduating from high school in 1988, Basich considered attending Santa Cruz College to study art, fashion design, or graphic design. Instead, with her parents' encouragement, she decided to skip college in order to pursue a career in the up-and-coming sport of snowboarding. "In my senior year, even though part of me wanted to go with the flow and follow my friends to the universities, I knew I would end up taking a different path," she said.

CAREER HIGHLIGHTS

Growing with the Sport

Tina Basich is widely viewed as one of the pioneers of women's snowboarding. She started competing in snowboarding contests in 1986, when the sport was just beginning to gain popularity. In these early days, she used duct tape to attach her moon boots to her board and padded her body with pizza boxes in case of a hard fall. Of course, she benefitted from

27

improvements in technology over the years. "As snowboarding grew we just sort of grew with it," she noted.

In 1988 — the year she graduated from high school — Basich received a sponsorship deal with the snowboard manufacturer Kemper that paid her $200 per month. She went on to win a slew of competitions over the next few years, including slalom races, halfpipe contests, and slopestyle competitions. In slalom races, competitors are timed as they race through a series of gates on a course. In halfpipe contests, competitors glide back and forth through a U-shaped tube of snow, gaining speed on the downward slopes and performing tricks at the top of the upward slopes. In slopestyle competitions, snowboarders perform a variety of tricks as they make their way through an obstacle course of jumps and rails. In 1994 Basich and her good friend Shannon Dunn became the first women snowboarders ever to receive their own signature professional snowboard models. Aimed at young women, these boards were shorter and narrower than typical men's models.

By the mid-1990s, when snowboarding was first featured in high-profile international events like the ESPN Winter X Games, Basich had already been involved in the sport for more than a decade. Weary from years of halfpipe competitions, she found herself longing to spend more time free-riding in the backcountry. In 1996 she decided to retire from competition in order to concentrate on making backcountry powder runs that could be filmed for television and video productions. "There just wasn't enough time to do everything. I stopped competing so I could push my limits free-riding," she explained. "Maybe the other reason I was over the halfpipe was my first-place finishes were getting harder to come by. The level of riding in the pipe among the new crop of girls was increasing and the competition was getting tougher. People were specializing in the pipe now and I was not into riding day-in and day-out pipe training. I had to explore the rest of the mountain, ride through the trees, check out natural chutes."

Specializing in Big Air

Basich's decision to retire from competition took her sponsors by surprise. They strongly advised her to make a more gradual transition to free-riding. In the meantime, the X Games introduced a new snowboarding event called Big Air. In this event, competitors make a single jump off of a large ramp and perform a complicated freestyle trick in mid-air. Basich adopted Big Air as her specialty, seeing it as a type of competition that would provide her with a new and exciting challenge. "There was something about a big-air event at the X Games that rang true for me," she recalled. "I knew I could do it because I liked catching big air off of cliffs in the backcountry, and while I wasn't getting a lot of film exposure yet, I did have a lot of still shots in magazines from some of my backcountry big airs. I was known for going for it."

In 1997 Basich finished third in Big Air and fourth in Slopestyle at the Winter X Games. She added a first-place finish in Big Air at the ESPN Freeride competition later that year. In 1998 she became the first woman ever to land a backside 720 (two complete flips in the air) in competition at the Winter X Games. This remarkable trick — which only a few top male snowboarders could perform successfully at that time — earned her an X Games gold medal. She described her award-winning performance in her autobiography: "I took three deep breaths and dropped onto the runway. In my head I repeated the words 'strong legs, strong legs.' The speed was fast and I launched off the jump, twisted my body to begin the rotation, spun around once very tight and fast, then went for another spin in the air. . . . My rotation was perfect, square to the mountain. I landed exactly where I had visualized it. I could not believe it. I could barely breathe. I had done it!" Basich added a second gold medal in Big Air on an artificial snow ramp at the 1998 Summer X Games.

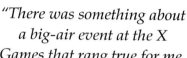

"There was something about a big-air event at the X Games that rang true for me. I knew I could do it because I liked catching big air off of cliffs in the backcountry."

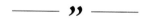

Basich's success in Big Air competitions continued in 1999, when she claimed first place in the MTV Snowed In Challenge. Her luck ran out a short time later, however, when she took a terrible fall while attempting her trademark 720 during a photo shoot at Mammoth Mountain, California. "I knew I was going too slow. I was already in the rotation of my 720, spinning as tightly as I could, wanting to get really small so maybe my spin would make up for my lack of speed. But I didn't even get my spin all the way around. It's a gut-wrenching feeling dangling in the air, just knowing I'm never going to make the landing, let alone the trick," she recalled in her autobiography. "I landed flat, on the top deck, all the air knocked from my lungs, missing the downhill slope of the landing by two feet. It all seemed so slow in the air, but it happened really fast. I crashed so hard — like hitting cement — that my body bounced like a rubber doll."

Basich ended up with severe fractures in her right ankle. Doctors performed surgery and inserted three screws to stabilize the joint. "That stopped me in

After winning an X Games Gold Medal in 1998, Basich changed her focus to tackling remote mountain ranges in Alaska and other parts of North America.

my tracks for a while," she remembered. "That was a bummer because, for the next six months, I was in my parents' recliner watching the hits from Blockbuster. I really learned a lot about myself and how my body heals. I used to feel like Superwoman. Now I take calculated risks only." In 2000, at the age of 30, Basich came back from her injury to place second in the Big

Air competition at the Sims Invitational World Snowboard Championships. It turned out to be her last major competition, as she finally followed through on her plan to concentrate on backcountry riding and other projects.

Focusing on Free-Riding and Other Opportunities

Since retiring from competition, Basich's career as a professional snowboarder has taken her in a number of different directions. She spends some of her time each year free-riding in remote locations for photo and film shoots. One of her favorite places to snowboard is Alaska. She particularly enjoys taking a helicopter to the top of an unknown peak to complete a "first descent"—become the first person ever to ride down that mountain. Of course, this type of "out-of-bounds" riding takes a healthy dose of courage. "Alaska is bigger than pictures can show—and there are huge risks," Basich admitted. "The mountain is always moving, cracks forming in the snow, avalanche sounds like low thunder in the distance, and the weather is constantly changing. . . . One thing that's clear in Alaska is that even if you do a first descent, the mountain is never your mountain. If you start thinking that way, Mother Nature has a way of smacking you across the face and humbling you to the size of a snowflake."

"One thing that's clear in Alaska is that even if you do a first descent, the mountain is never your mountain. If you start thinking that way, Mother Nature has a way of smacking you across the face and humbling you to the size of a snowflake."

On one video shoot in Alaska, for example, Basich narrowly missed becoming caught in an avalanche. As she rode down a slope, a huge crack formed in the snow beneath her board. She quickly moved to the right and made it to the escape route that she had plotted out earlier. Three months later, she was shocked to see the film footage of her near tragedy. "In the film you can see this whole mountain moving with snow, pluming over cliffs as it travels down the chute," she recalled. "And there I am, this little speck in the frame waiting over to the right above some rocks, watching it all happen. It was scary to watch and it brought chills and made me nervous all over again. I had no idea it was that big of a slide. Alaska can make you feel so small and then in the next instant, after an incredible run, you can feel bigger than life."

In 2001 Basich started writing a book about her life and career. "My parents moved and I started to pack up all my stuff and realized how many photos and how many great times I've had," she remembered. "Snowboarding has been such a big and important part of my life, so I really wanted to bring all that together." She spent the next year and a half working on the book, which was published in 2003 as *Pretty Good for a Girl: The Autobiography of a Snowboarding Pioneer.* "It's kinda like my journal," she noted. "It has all my adventure stories. It is definitely a reflection of my life. It includes all the key points that moved me or changed me, basically the most important points in my life. I hope the book to be inspiring the not-so-normal path in life."

Aimed at aspiring snowboarders, the book includes advice sections that cover topics ranging from choosing a snowboard and stretching to prevent injury to finding a sponsor and surviving an avalanche. "I have learned so much from traveling and all of my experiences in snowboarding and being in the backcountry," Basich explained. "So I felt like I wanted to share those and pass them along to the next person that might be interested in it."

As snowboarding has gained more mainstream appeal in recent years, Basich's stature as one of the sports' true pioneers has made her a sought-after figure for commercials, interviews, TV appearances, and awards presentations. She co-starred in the action-sports documentary film *Keep Your Eyes Open,* and she was featured in the X Games Pro Boarder video game. "I'm a character in that game, which is so weird — to see yourself animated," she said. "I can do 900s [two and a half flips] now! It's cool — I don't have to beat myself up."

In 2003 Basich became the host of a new sports adventure show called "GKA (girls kick a\$\$)" on Fuel TV, a division of Fox Sports Network. "It's a girls' action sports show that will showcase all the female great athletes in snowboarding, skateboarding, surfing, motocross, and things like that," she explained. "My show gives all the girls a platform to show what girls can do in action sports."

Serving as a Role Model for Women Snowboarders

Although some longtime snowboarders resented the sport's transition from alternative to mainstream, Basich welcomed the change and all the opportunities it brought her. "Everyone who was involved in snowboarding when it boomed was a little reserved about it. It was changing so fast we didn't know what to think," she noted. "But I embrace it, because more people are having fun with snowboarding. . . . And because it's mainstream, I still can be a pro snowboarder and have this be my career."

In 2003 Basich published Pretty Good for a Girl, *a memoir of her experiences in snowboarding's early years.*

Basich enjoys being a role model for young women just entering the sport of snowboarding. She encourages women to get involved, even if they never plan to bust moves in the halfpipe. "Women make great snowboarders. We have the grace and balance you need," she stated. "I think the extreme image of the sport may be the attractive part. If women see the X Games, even if they are not going to do that themselves, in a way they are a part of it and can say, 'Yeah, I snowboard,' when somebody asks. That's something to be proud of."

For young women who want to perform tricks and perhaps attract a sponsor, Basich offers the following advice: "Get a season pass and ride as much as possible. The way people get good at snowboarding is they go many days in a winter. You're not going to get better by going on your two trips a winter for 14 years. If you get 50 days in every winter, you're going to be advancing. If you're bustin' tricks at a park, there's probably someone at that mountain who lives there and who's a professional snowboarder. They know the rep, who can hook you up with a board, and then you get noticed by the company, and all of a sudden the company is calling you. Contests are also a great place to show off and get noticed."

HOME AND FAMILY

When she is not traveling the world with her snowboard, Basich lives in Lake Tahoe, California. "I'm a homebody that travels," she noted. "When I'm out I miss my home, and when I'm home I want to travel." She is handy around the house and enjoys completing home-improvement projects. "I'm a project girl," she admitted. "I live in an old house and my mom and dad got me a pink tool set and pink tool belt. I've been building a picket fence."

Basich remains single, although she has been involved in several high-profile relationships over the years. She dated Dave Grohl, lead singer for the Foo Fighters, for two years before the relationship ended. "Breakups suck," she stated. "Rock star breakups suck the worst." She eventually hopes to settle down and start a family. "Hopefully, I will be married and have little snowboarding kiddies," she said.

Basich remains close to her parents, who have always supported her and her brother in their careers as professional snowboarders. "I have been so lucky," she noted. "They are so supportive. I think they just saw how passionate my brother and I were about doing it. It gave us so much confidence."

Basich (right) is a founding member of Boarding for Breast Cancer, a nonprofit organization that raises money for breast cancer research.

HOBBIES AND OTHER INTERESTS

Although Basich loves snowboarding, she is careful to cultivate other interests in her life. For example, she is an accomplished artist who provides a painting every year for the graphics on her signature snowboard. She also helps her sponsors design snowboard clothing and gear. "I could easily see myself getting burnt-out if I snowboarded every day in the winter," she explained. "So I snowboard a couple of days, and then I'll do artwork, paint, and hang out with friends. Then it will snow again, and I'll be on for another five days, and then I'll rest and go visit my family or whatever. I don't fill up my whole winter with just snowboarding."

Basich is also active in charity work. She is a founding member of Boarding for Breast Cancer (B4BC), a nonprofit organization that has raised over a million dollars for breast cancer research and education since 1996. The group raises money by putting on snowboarding contests and musical concerts. Its goal is to increase breast cancer awareness in young women and emphasize the importance of early detection. "I was one of about five girls who founded it because we lost a girlfriend of ours who was our age to breast cancer [snowboarder Monica Steward, who was diagnosed with the disease at age 26 and died two years later]," Basich related. "We've raised lots of money and hopefully raised lots of awareness. Everybody comes out, listens to music, snowboards, and gets together for a good cause."

WRITINGS

Pretty Good for a Girl: The Autobiography of a Snowboarding Pioneer, 2003 (with Kathleen Gasperini)

AWARDS AND HONORS

ESPN Freeride Competition, Big Air: 1997, gold medal
Winter X Games, Big Air: 1998, gold medal
Summer X Games, Big Air: 1998, gold medal
MTV Snowed In, Big Air: 1999, gold medal
Sims Invitational World Snowboard Championships, Big Air: 2000, silver medal

FURTHER READING

Books

Basich, Tina, with Kathleen Gasperini. *Pretty Good for a Girl: The Autobiography of a Snowboarding Pioneer,* 2003

Periodicals

Denver Rocky Mountain News, Jan. 29, 2004, p.D14
Los Angeles Times, Nov. 4, 2003, p.F11
Miami Herald, Sep. 28, 2003, p.D19
Oregonian, Oct. 10, 2003, Arts and Living, p.7
Sacramento Bee, Jan. 23, 2004, p.E3
Seattle Post-Intelligencer, Sep. 27, 2003

Online Articles

http://www.944.biz/sandiego
(*San Diego 944 Magazine,* "Tina Basich: Pretty Good for a Girl," Feb. 17, 2004)
http://sportsillustrated.cnn.com/siforwomen/2001/january_february/gear_goddess
(*Sports Illustrated for Women,* "Gear Goddess: Queen of the Board," Dec. 28, 2000)

http://classic.mountainzone.com/snowboarding/99/features
  (*Classic Mountain Zone,* "An Interview with Tina Basich," 1999)
http://www.ugo.com/channels/sports/features
  (*Ugo.com,* "Tina Basich," undated)
http://www.powderroom.net/profiles
  Powderroom.net, "Tina Basich," undated)

ADDRESS

Tina Basich
HarperCollins Publishers Inc.
10 East 53rd Street
New York, NY 10022

WORLD WIDE WEB SITES

http://expn.go.com/athletes/bios
http://www.b4bc.org

Sasha Cohen 1984-

American Figure Skater
Silver Medalist in the 2004 World Figure Skating
Championships

BIRTH

Alexandra Pauline Cohen, known by the nickname Sasha, was
born on October 26, 1984, in Westwood, California. "Sasha is
the Russian nickname for Alexandra," she explained. "When I
was four or five, I couldn't spell Alexandra. It had too many
letters. So when I went to school I told them my name is
Sasha."

Sasha's father, Roger Cohen, works as an attorney in California. Her mother, Galina Cohen, is a homemaker. Galina was born in Ukraine—a nation in Eastern Europe that was once part of the former Soviet Union—and immigrated to the United States as a teenager. Russian is her native language, and she often uses it when speaking to Sasha and her younger sister, Natasha. Although Sasha can understand Russian completely, she cannot speak it fluently.

YOUTH

Sasha comes from an athletic family. Her mother participated in both gymnastics and ballet during her childhood in Ukraine. Her maternal grandfather was such a talented gymnast that he once performed for Joseph Stalin, who was the leader of the Soviet Union from 1922 through 1953. Sasha began taking gymnastics lessons at the age of five, and within two years she had reached Level 5 in the sport. (American amateur gymnasts are classified according to skill from Level 1 to Level 10, with 10 being the highest.) Before long, however, she decided to apply her athletic ability to a different sport.

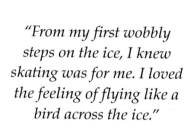

"From my first wobbly steps on the ice, I knew skating was for me. I loved the feeling of flying like a bird across the ice."

When Sasha was seven years old, a friend from her gymnastics class invited her to an ice skating party. "From my first wobbly steps on the ice," she recalled, "I knew skating was for me. I loved the feeling of flying like a bird across the ice." Sasha enjoyed it so much that she asked her parents if she could take figure skating lessons. Although her parents agreed, they never expected her to become a professional skater. Since most professional skaters start at a much younger age—typically about four or five years old—Sasha was considered a bit old to be starting lessons. "That couple of years can make a big difference," she acknowledged. "It meant that I had to catch up."

As it turned out, Sasha's figure skating skills developed very quickly and she had no trouble catching up with her peers. She learned the basics after about a year of group skating lessons. By the time she made her first single-axel jump, she was hooked. In an axel, the skater starts the jump facing forward on the left skate, rotates one-and-a-half times in the air, and lands traveling backward on the right foot. It is considered the most difficult jump in figure skating. Once Sasha mastered it, she was eager to try more and more difficult jumps. By the time she was 10 years old, she was successfully completing such maneuvers as double salchows and double toe loops. "Sasha didn't start out to be a competitive skater. She was into a lot of different things," her mother recalled. "But she's just a competitive kid. I think it's something you have to be born with."

EDUCATION

At the age of 10, Cohen committed to skating full time. Since she spent five hours per day on the ice, she completed her schooling through a combination of public and private schools and tutors. Beginning at the age of 15, she attended Futures High School, a private institution in Mission Viejo, California, where she received one-on-one instruction from teachers. She attended Aliso Niguel High School during her senior year. Despite her demanding practice and travel schedule, she was a straight-A student and earned her high school diploma in 2002. She later took nutrition classes through Penn State University's world campus program.

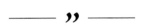

"While other kids were hanging out and having fun, I worked on my skating," Cohen acknowledged. "I gave up a lot, but I was driven to skate so it wasn't a hard choice for me. I wanted to be out there on the ice."

Cohen recognized that her desire to be a competitive skater required her to make some sacrifices. "While other kids were hanging out and having fun, I worked on my skating," she acknowledged. "I gave up a lot, but I was driven to skate so it wasn't a hard choice for me. I wanted to be out there on the ice."

CAREER HIGHLIGHTS

Making a Name for Herself

When Cohen was 12 years old, she started training under John Nicks. A former Olympic pairs figure skater, Nicks had coached top U.S. skating competitors since the early 1960s. Under Nicks's guidance, Cohen quickly moved up through the levels of figure skating competition. In 1999 she finished second among junior skaters at the U.S. National Championships. Her strong performance helped her earn a spot on the United States Figure Skating Association (USFSA) team for 1999-2000. The USFSA is the governing body for the sport in the United States.

Cohen and coach John Nicks react to posted scores after her performance in the short program at the 2000 U.S. Figure Skating Championships.

Cohen first gained widespread attention in February 2000, when she earned a silver medal in the senior division at the U.S. Figure Skating Championships. "That one moment totally changed my life—and my skating career," Cohen remembered. "I started getting fan mail from people I'd never met. I was even stopped for an autograph. . . . Before the U.S.

41

Championships, no one outside of figure skating had really heard of me. Suddenly, I was a celebrity."

As the world began watching Cohen on the ice, many observers praised her grace and artistry. While she possessed the athletic ability to perform difficult jumps and spins, she managed to do so while holding her body in positions that were striking for their beauty and originality. For example, she came up with a move that became known as the "Sasha curl," in which she tipped her head back while curling one leg up behind her — so that her skate blade touched her ponytail — without using her hands. "She's very elegant," Nicks noted. "We call her the 'china doll.' She has a wonderful flexibility and is a very precise skater. She can carry a classical music piece, and many girls aren't able to do that."

Soon after the U.S. Championships in 2000, Cohen flew to Germany to compete in the Junior World Championships. She was very excited to compete in such a prestigious international event. "When I won the silver medal, it was just for the U.S.," she explained. "But this one was for the world! It was also huge for my career because I had to place in the top three at this competition before I could qualify to skate in the Senior World Championships against future Olympians. But I knew I was ready to move up — all I had to do was get another medal."

Unfortunately, when Cohen arrived in Germany she was not in top mental and physical condition. First, she was disappointed when her father and sister were not able to accompany her to the competition. Then she experienced a long delay in getting from the airport to her hotel because of a snowstorm and a traffic accident. Forced to compete on only a few hours of sleep, Cohen fell twice during her performance and placed sixth. "I kept thinking that I only needed to place in the top three. Now I realize that was the wrong attitude," she recalled. "My chance to go to the Senior Worlds was over. I was unbelievably disappointed in myself. I had let all of my fans down. It was horrible."

Battling Injuries and Controversy

Shortly after returning from Germany, Cohen suffered a stress fracture in her lower back. She felt something pop in her back during a training session, and then she had trouble performing some of her moves. The problem grew worse for several months, until the injury was finally diagnosed in December of that year. Nicks suggested that she take a break from skating so that her injury could heal. But Cohen ignored his advice and continued to practice. She was determined to work through the pain so that she could compete in the U.S. Figure Skating Championships in January 2001. "She resists me on a permanent basis," her coach said. "One part of my philosophy is to create an athlete who's independent, not dependent, to create someone who's courageous and has a determined point of view. I've created this monster, and it's come back to haunt me."

Even though one of Cohen's doctors told her that skating would cause no further damage to her back, her condition gradually worsened to the point that she could not even complete her routine during practice. She finally gave in to her pain and withdrew from the U.S. Championships. After several months of recovery, Cohen was ready to return to competition. "I never thought I couldn't come back," she stated. "I knew it would be hard, but I always persevered, even when I was frustrated, and I worked really hard."

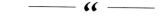

Upon returning to competition in September 2001, Cohen finished fourth at the Goodwill Games. The following month she competed in her first international event at the senior level and won the Finlandia Trophy. A few weeks later, at the Skate America Competition in Colorado Springs, Colorado, Cohen attempted to become the first woman to land a quadruple salchow in this difficult maneuver, the skater travels backward across the ice, takes off from the back

"I never thought I couldn't come back," Cohen stated. "I knew it would be hard, but I always persevered, even when I was frustrated, and I worked really hard."

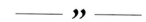

inside edge of one skate, does four complete turns in the air, and lands on the back outside edge of the other skate. Unfortunately, Cohen failed to complete the quadruple salchow during her routine, and she finished a disappointing fifth in the competition.

As the 2002 U.S. Figure Skating Championships approached, some observers wondered whether Cohen might be poised to unseat Michelle Kwan—a six-time U.S. national champion and 1998 Olympic silver medalist—as America's top female skater. Experts acknowledged that Cohen had not yet matched Kwan's knack for giving terrific performances under pressure. But many observers felt that Cohen's combination of grace and skill made her the most likely threat to Kwan's reign. "I try not to think about it that way," Cohen said of the supposed rivalry with Kwan. "For me, the competition has to be between me and myself—between the skater I am now and the skater I would like to become. I don't want to 'dethrone' Michelle."

The U.S. Championships gained added importance that year because the top three finishers would earn the chance to represent the country at the 2002 Winter Olympic Games in Salt Lake City, Utah. Cohen hoped to improve upon her silver medal performance in 2000 and prove that she was fully recovered from the injury that forced her to miss the event in 2001.

On the day of the competition, though, Cohen became the center of a strange controversy. Several reporters and skating fans accused her of intentionally skating too close to Kwan during warm-up exercises. Cohen denied that she had tried to harm or intimidate her rival. She claimed that their near-collision was simply a result of too many skaters trying to warm up at the same time. "In the whole six minutes, we were close once. A whole bunch of other skaters had close calls as well," she explained. "I know that I was fine and just going to get my stuff in. It's just something people chose to talk about, and hopefully it will die down."

Cohen overcame the fuss to claim the silver medal at the U.S. Championships, while Kwan went on to win the gold medal. Sarah Hughes finished in third place to fill the final spot on the U.S. Olympic Team. "Of the three women, Sasha was the only one to perform moves I had never seen before," said Paul Wylie, who won a silver medal in men's figure skating at the 1992 Games. "It's a great thing to surprise the audience."

Competing in the 2002 Olympic Games

As the 2002 Winter Olympics approached, Cohen received a great deal of media attention. Many experts thought she had an excellent chance of winning a gold medal in Salt Lake City. "I think Sasha Cohen is just as capable of going in [to the Olympics] and winning as anyone, depending on other people's performances," said Sandra Bezic, a choreographer who worked with former Olympic skaters such as Kristi Yamaguchi, Tara Lipinski, and Brian Boitano. "She's fantastic, and I thought her choreography in both her programs [at the U.S. National Championships] was perfect for her stage of development. It was all just excellent work." Peggy Fleming, the 1968 Olympic figure skating gold medalist, added that "she's very ambitious and fearless and breathtakingly beautiful. The way she can move is amazing."

Cohen expressed cautious optimism when asked about her chances in the Olympics. "Doing well at Nationals is a really big step for me, and we'll see what happens now at Salt Lake," she stated. "I go in with a dream of winning Olympic gold, and I'm thinking more of something I can do for myself, and that's to skate two clean programs."

Cohen competing at the 2002 Winter Olympics in Salt Lake City, Utah.

The Olympic figure skating competition consists of two events: the short program, which accounts for one-third of a competitor's final score; and the long program, which accounts for two-thirds of the final score. Cohen performed well in the short program. She finished the first portion of the

45

competition in third place and found herself in strong contention for a medal. Unfortunately, Cohen made several mistakes during her long program and dropped to fourth place. She was disappointed that she did not win a medal. "A lot of people thought I did well," she said. "But it wasn't my personal best and I was disappointed with that. There will always be a little bit of regret, a little bit of hurt, that I felt that was an opportunity I didn't take." The American team still managed a strong showing, however, with Hughes claiming the gold medal for women's figure skating and Kwan taking the bronze.

Switching Coaches

After the Olympics, Cohen did not take a break from the sport. She performed in the Tom Collins Champions on Ice tour and trained hard for the 2002 World Championships. Though she entered this major international competition with high expectations, Cohen placed fourth. Her disappointment led her to rethink various aspects of her career, including her choice of coach.

In November 2002, after training under John Nicks for over six years, Cohen decided that she was ready for a change. "It was really hard to leave Mr. Nicks," she admitted. "He was my coach since intermediates. As a person, it was hard to imagine anyone else putting me on the ice, but I realized for my skating to progress, I really needed a higher level of training." One factor in her decision was the lack of personal attention she received on the ice. "I just didn't feel like the training conditions were what I needed," she explained. "I was on the ice for two 45-minute sessions with 15 or 20 kids. It was more of a social environment."

Cohen and her family flew to Connecticut to meet with Nikolai Morozov and Tatiana Tarasova for some help with choreography. After working with them, Cohen decided to hire them as her coaches. Within two weeks, she and her family packed up their household and moved across the country to Connecticut. Since her father still practiced law in California, he commuted between the two states. Shortly after Cohen joined them, Morozov and Tarasova split up. Cohen stayed with Tarasova, a Russian former gymnast who had coached more than 40 Olympic or world champions, including the 2002 Olympic men's figure skating gold medalist, Alexei Yagudin.

Cohen was very pleased with the training she received from Tarasova. "I couldn't ask any more in a coach," she noted. "The way she trains me, I have 110 percent trust in everything she does. We have a real plan every single day." The change seemed to pay off immediately for Cohen. She won several international competitions over the next few months, including Skate Canada and the Trophee Lalique in France, and she also placed second at the Cup of Russia competition. "I feel when I'm training with Tatiana I'm a lot more prepared for competition," Cohen explained. "Tatiana expects more out of me than I expect of myself." For her part, Tarasova expressed great confidence in Cohen's future. "Sasha is something special. She is the most talented skater I've ever seen," Tarasova stated. "I think she has 10 times more to show than she is showing right now."

With each competition, Cohen's desire to win became stronger. "You want it to be perfect every time, and sometimes it can't be," she said. "I'm hard on myself. I want everything to be perfect all the time. I want to be the No. 1 skater. I want to be the best in the world." At the U.S. National Championships in early 2003, however, Cohen placed third behind Michelle Kwan and Sarah Hughes. She was so disappointed with herself that she burst into tears at the post-event news conference. A few months later, she suffered another disappointment when she finished fourth at the 2003 World Figure Skating Championships. "I was letting the pressure get to me," she explained. "Now I'm trying not to do that anymore."

With each competition, Cohen's desire to win became stronger. "You want it to be perfect every time, and sometimes it can't be," she said. "I'm hard on myself. I want everything to be perfect all the time. I want to be the No. 1 skater. I want to be the best in the world."

Later that year, however, Cohen posted impressive victories in several smaller competitions. In October she won the Campbell's International Figure Skating Classic, beating Kwan for the first time in her career. She went on to win Skate America and successfully defend her titles at Skate Canada and Trophee Lalique.

Switching Coaches Again

Although Cohen won eight gold medals with Tarasova as her coach, all of the major prizes in figure skating—the Olympics, World Championships, and National Championships—continued to elude her. So in December 2003 Cohen surprised many observers by changing coaches yet again. Just two weeks before the 2004 U.S. Figure Skating Championships, Cohen announced that she would begin working with Robin Wagner, who is best

Cohen is consoled by her coach Robin Wagner at the 2004 World Figure Skating Championships. Leading going into the final, Cohen was edged out for the gold medal by Shizuka Arakawa and had to settle for silver.

known for coaching Olympic gold medalist Sarah Hughes. Cohen and her parents had met Wagner in 1997 and maintained a friendship. When the Cohens decided that Sasha needed a new coach, Tarasova recommended Wagner. "She was our first choice, and we're very lucky this could all come together," Cohen's mother said.

Cohen began commuting from Connecticut to New York, staying with Wagner until she could find a place of her own in the city. As soon as she began working with Wagner, Cohen knew that she had made the right decision. For one thing, Wagner put on skates and went out on the ice with Cohen during their training sessions. This style of coaching was different from most other coaches, who usually watch their skaters from the sides of the rink. Cohen also noted that she and Wagner had a certain chemistry. "She's brought a lot of the joy back into my skating, like when I was eight years old," she stated. "We just click."

Cohen and Wagner worked very hard to prepare for the U.S. Championships in January 2004. Once again, though, Cohen fell just short of her goal of winning a major competition. She won the silver medal at the national championships, placing second behind Kwan.

In March 2004 Cohen competed in the World Skating Championships in Dortmund, Germany. She turned in a terrific performance in the early going, only to be nosed out for the gold in the free skating segment of the competition. Ironically, the winner of the gold medal was Japan's Shizuka Arakawa, who had hired Tarasova as her coach after Cohen left. "It's a little funny with all the coaching switches going around," Cohen said. "Everyone has to find what works for them."

Aiming for the 2006 Winter Olympics

Although Cohen has yet to win a major international competition, her consistently strong finishes have ensured that she will be considered among the favorites to medal at the 2006 Winter Olympic Games. She took a break from competitive skating following the 2004 World Championships and joined the Champions on Ice tour. Even though touring was hard work, she enjoyed skating to please the crowd and herself rather than a panel of judges. "We still get up early and spend a lot of time at the rink," she explained. "I guess the bottom line is that it will make me better when I go back to competition. But right now, I'm having a lot of fun. . . . The work is for my body; the fun is for my brain."

In addition to training on the ice, Cohen also spends several hours each week in ballet class, stretching class, or Pilates class. (Pilates is a form of exercise that helps improve strength and flexibility.) Her discipline has helped her become one of the most original and artistic skaters in the world. "Everyone has their strengths," she noted. "For some people it's jumping. For others it's spinning. The ballet has really helped me do what I do best."

Cohen has attracted legions of fans over the course of her long career. She is proud of the fact that she serves as a role model for many younger skaters. "It's a lot of fun to be a role model," she stated. "It's also inspiring to me." "I don't think she's really aware of how far-reaching [her populari-

Cohen has her sights set on a gold medal in the 2006 Winter Olympics.

ty] is," her mother added. "But she's always tried to be a good role model. She's a very hard worker—she doesn't sit around chatting. She makes the most out of every day."

HOME AND FAMILY

Cohen, who is single, lives with her family in New York City. "It's just gorgeous every time we see the skyline of Manhattan," she said. "You get the sense of excitement. And I have such an amazing appreciation for New York City." She shares her home with a dog named Mocha and two cats named Mia and Meow.

HOBBIES AND OTHER INTERESTS

When Cohen is not skating, she enjoys cooking and baking. She also enjoys reading, shopping, making jewelry, and hanging out with her friends. "I'll only have free time on the weekends," she admitted. "Most of my friends are skaters, but I do have friends who don't skate. But it's hard work to keep in touch. To be a really good skater, you have to work hard and you really have to love it."

> "It's a lot of fun to be a role model," Cohen said. "It's also inspiring to me."

Cohen is also involved in several charity organizations. She is a strong supporter of the Connecticut Children's Medical Center and acts as a spokesperson for Girls, Inc. and Covenant House. She is also active in the Soldiers' Angels program, which sponsors military personnel who serve in foreign countries.

HONORS AND AWARDS

U.S. National Figure Skating Championships: silver medal, 2000; silver medal, 2002; bronze medal, 2003; silver medal, 2004
Olympic Women's Figure Skating: fourth place, 2002
Women of Achievement in Sports Award: 2003
World Figure Skating Championships: silver medal, 2004
Skater of the Year (*Skating Magazine*): 2004

FURTHER READING

Books

Who's Who in America, 2004

Periodicals

Boston Globe, Jan. 19, 2001, p.E1
Denver Rocky Mountain News, Apr. 20, 2004, p.C14
Los Angeles Times, Feb. 3, 2002, Sports, p.1; Nov. 4, 2002, Sports, p.13
New York Times, Sep. 26, 2003, p.D4
Orange County (Calif.) Register, Feb. 9, 2000, p.D1
Sports Illustrated for Kids, Jan. 1, 2004, p.46
Sports Illustrated for Women, Mar./Apr. 2000, p.68
Teen, Nov. 2000, p.64
Washington Post, Jan. 11, 2003, p.D10; Jan. 7, 2004, p.D3

ADDRESS

Sasha Cohen
c/o www.sashacohen.com
132 Waterford Park Drive
Greer, SC 29650

WORLD WIDE WEB SITES

http://www.sashacohen.com
http://www.usfigureskating.org

Dale Earnhardt, Jr. 1974-
American Professional Race Car Driver
Winner of the 2004 NASCAR Daytona 500

BIRTH

Dale Earnhardt, Jr., was born on October 10, 1974, in Kannap-
olis, North Carolina. His parents were Dale Earnhardt, Sr., a
professional race car driver, and his second wife, Brenda. Dale
Jr. has a sister, Kelley, as well as two half-siblings from his father's other marriages. He has an older half-brother, Kerry,
who was the son of Earnhardt, Sr., and his first wife, Latane.
Dale Jr. also has a younger half-sister, Taylor, who was born to
Earnhardt, Sr., and his third wife, Teresa.

Dale Jr.'s family is one of the most famous in American racing history. His grandfather, Ralph Earnhardt, was a NASCAR (National Association of Stock Car Auto Racing) champion in the late model division, and his father was a seven-time NASCAR Winston Cup champion. In addition, his maternal grandfather, Robert Gee, was a highly regarded NASCAR mechanic and fabricator. Finally, his half-brother Kerry is a fixture on the NASCAR Busch Series circuit.

YOUTH

During Earnhardt's early childhood, he and his sister Kelley were raised by their mom after her divorce from their father. Earnhardt Sr. was an emerging star on the NASCAR circuit by the late 1970s, and he made only occasional efforts to maintain a relationship with his children. (For more information, see *Biography Today,* Apr. 2001.) "I only saw my dad once or twice a year," confirmed Earnhardt. "I was too young to know what he was doing, although I guess I was kind of curious. Then one night [in 1980] the kitchen caught on fire and the house burned down. My mother went to live with her parents and I ended up at Dad's house."

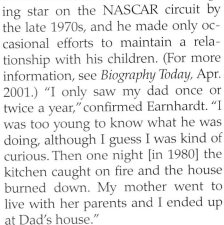

"Dad was away racing most of the time," recalled Earnhardt. "He was so focused on winning that even when he was at home between races, his mind was still at the racetrack instead of at home with us."

Earnhardt spent the rest of his youth in Mooresville, North Carolina, a town about 30 miles north of Charlotte where his father operated his racing shop. But he still did not see a lot of Dale Sr. "Dad was away racing most of the time," recalled Earnhardt. "He was so focused on winning that even when he was at home between races, his mind was still at the racetrack instead of at home with us."

As a result, Earnhardt was raised by a combination of people. His stepmother Teresa was an important presence in his life, but she often accompanied his father to races and left Dale Jr. in the care of nannies. He also credits his older sister Kelley with much of his upbringing. "She could always handle things, so I went to her for everything," he said.

Earnhardt's mother also remained an important part of his life, but their get-togethers were always bittersweet. "She'd come for a weekend, and we'd stay with her at some crummy-ass hotel," he recalled. "When she left, she'd cry. It tore us up. I love my mother. That's why it took me a long time to have a relationship with Teresa. I didn't give her a lot of respect."

A Troubled Adolescence

As a youngster, Earnhardt—who also became known in his family by the nicknames "Junior" and "Little E"—endured a lot of teasing and bullying from other kids. Jealous of his father's fame and wealth, they ridiculed him whenever Earnhardt Sr. crashed or ran poorly. "Kids bullied him," admitted his sister Kelley. "He was a lot smaller than they were. He was shy and sensitive and easily intimidated. He didn't stand up for himself. I never thought he'd race cars."

The teasing was made worse by the fact that Earnhardt's relationship with his father remained a distant one. Unable to connect with his father and his passion for racing, he spent much of his time alone in his room playing on the computer. "Dad was strict," recalled Kelley. "We couldn't have kids come over to spend the night. We never sat down as a family to dinner. We didn't get everything we wanted. For fifteen years, we had a 13-inch black-and-white TV."

> **"**
>
> *"Kids bullied him," admitted Earnhardt's sister Kelley. "He was a lot smaller than they were. He was shy and sensitive and easily intimidated. He didn't stand up for himself. I never thought he'd race cars."*
>
> **"**

Earnhardt did make periodic attempts to explore his father's world of racing. At age 12, for instance, he started racing go-karts. "Dad thought racing a kart would be fun, so I got one and went out to set the world in fire," Earnhardt recalled. "But karts don't have roll cages or seat belts, so most of the time I was being run over by or thrown off my own kart."

As he grew older, Earnhardt also accompanied his parents to some of the NASCAR events across the United States. But these trips gave him little opportunity to establish a closer relationship with his father. "The races were on Sundays mostly and were all over the country, and even if we went and even if my dad won, he'd usually be fuming about something somebody did to him in the race," said Earnhardt. "Sometimes he'd come back home from somewhere in the country, after he won a race, and he'd get on another plane to go hunting somewhere."

By his mid-teens Earnhardt had turned angry and resentful, a self-described "bad kid" who "lied to my parents and didn't do as I was told." But it was also around this time that his love for racing first began to blossom. Or, as he once put it, he realized that he would "never forge a relationship" with his father if he did not race.

At age 17, Earnhardt and his older half-brother Kerry (who he met for the first time only a couple years earlier) pooled their money to buy a 1978 Monte Carlo at a junkyard. They rebuilt it themselves with Kelley's help, then took turns driving it in local races. After their first season, Earnhardt Sr. offered to buy cars for all three kids to race. The next few years were a lot of fun for Junior. "We'd go down to Myrtle Beach [in South Carolina] — it was about a four-hour drive — race and drive back," Earnhardt recalled. "We did that for three years. Some nights Kerry would be at one track, Kelley at another one, and me at a third one. I ran 119 late-model races and never won, but I was in the top five over 80 times. Dad . . . noticed that I always brought the car home in one piece. I rarely tore it up. In those four years, he never saw me race once, but he always kept an eye on how the car looked when I got home."

Earnhardt admits, though, that his older sister was the best driver among the younger generation of Earnhardts. "Rumors still float around that Kelley was the most promising driver among the three of us, and I'm not afraid to say that, yes, Kelley was the best of us kids by far," he wrote in *Driver #8,* a memoir of his 2000 NASCAR season. "She was tough as nails and did the most with little help or cash behind her."

EDUCATION

Earnhardt attended elementary school in Mooresville. By the time he reached high school, his parents became so fed up with his increasingly rebellious behavior that they sent him to a military school. He was kicked out of the military school, but he finally graduated from a Christian school at age 18.

During his high school years, Earnhardt's father repeatedly told him that his biggest regret was dropping out of school in ninth grade. He stressed to Junior and his other children how important it was for them to get a good education. "Education, yeah, it was such a big thing," Earnhardt recalled sourly. "So I graduated high school, and where was my father? He didn't come to graduation. He was in a race somewhere. I understand now, of course, but I was looking forward to holding that diploma in his face. Except he wasn't there. He was at some other end of the earth."

After high school, Junior and Kerry moved into a trailer across the street from their father's racing headquarters. Earnhardt then enrolled at nearby

Earnhardt made a big splash on the Busch circuit, claiming two consecutive national championships.

Mitchell Community College, where he earned an automotive degree after two years.

CAREER HIGHLIGHTS

After earning his degree from Mitchell, Earnhardt went to work at a Chevrolet dealership in Newton, North Carolina, that was owned by his father. He soon became known as the fastest oil-change man in the shop. He took great pride in this distinction, and he still looks back fondly on his days as a mechanic. "[I loved] eating with the guys, the camaraderie, Christmas parties," he explained. "Everyone was real, as opposed to famous people who don't know who their friends are. If I ever left racing, I'd go back to being a mechanic. It was a good, honest job."

By the mid-1990s, however, Earnhardt had become convinced that he actually had a talent for the sport of auto racing. He felt that his best attributes were superior track vision and an ability to keep his cool even during the most intense and unpredictable race situations. "Some guys get confused, disoriented easily," he explained. "I was able to focus on what I was doing. I saw other drivers lose their composure and get frustrated, but I was good at maintaining my composure."

Joining the Busch Circuit

In 1996 Earnhardt began to compete in NASCAR's Busch Grand National Series. The Busch Series is the second highest NASCAR division, after the Nextel Cup (known as the Winston Cup until the 2004 season). Although it is not as prestigious as the Nextel Cup circuit, it is still wildly popular with NASCAR fans. They recognize that drivers who excel in the Busch Series usually go on to become stars at the next level.

> "I wanted to impress [my dad]," Earnhardt acknowledged. "I could have went and done other things, but no matter how successful I'd been . . . it wouldn't have been as impressive to him as winning a race."

Earnhardt participated in his first-ever Busch Series race in Myrtle Beach, where he had competed numerous times in smaller races over the previous few years. He finished the race in 14th place. In 1997 he raced in eight more Busch Series events, posting one top-ten finish. Throughout this time, he continued to see racing as a way to establish a closer relationship with his famous father. "I wanted to impress him," he acknowledged. "I could have went and done other things, but no matter how successful I'd been . . . it wouldn't have been as impressive to him as winning a race."

By 1998 Earnhardt's skills had progressed to the point that his father offered him the opportunity to race in Busch Grand National Series competition for his team, Dale Earnhardt Inc. (DEI). When Junior accepted the offer, he gained access to one of the most impressive NASCAR operations in the country. Noting that the DEI facility sprawls over 360 acres of Mooresville countryside, Earnhardt says that "the shop looks more like NASA [the National Aeronautics and Space Administration] than anything else. . . . DEI isn't just for testing, building, and working on cars. There are offices, conference rooms, a museum, an auto showroom, a gift shop, and an executive dining room (known as the Trophy Room) with big, heavy, furniture and rich, dark paneling just like you would expect to find at an investment banking firm. But that's the kind of money that my dad — and NASCAR — has generated."

Earnhardt (right) enjoyed a much closer relationship with his father, Dale Sr. (left), after he began auto racing himself.

Racing in the number 8 car—the same number his grandfather used—Earnhardt turned in dominating performances throughout the 1998 campaign. He won his first Busch Series race at the Texas Motor Speedway outside of Fort Worth. As he recalls, his father "[talked] to me on the radio throughout the race. He was so happy in the winner's circle I could hardly believe it. From then on, I wanted to keep winning just to see how happy it made him."

Earnhardt won six more races before the 1998 season was through, enabling him to cruise to the Busch Series championship. (Throughout the Busch and Nextel series seasons, drivers earn points based on their finishing position in races, number of pole positions earned, laps led in races, and other criteria; at the end of each year, the drivers with the most points

59

in the divisions for the season are named the NASCAR Busch Series and Nextel Cup champions.) Earnhardt took great pride in the championship, noting that "I became the first third-generation driver to win a major NASCAR title."

Two-Time Champ

Despite his championship, the late 1990s were not an altogether happy time for Earnhardt. "I had problems driving for my father," he said. "I didn't get much respect as a driver from his employees. I was the SOB, Son of the Boss." He also was angered by other NASCAR teams' suggestions that his success was due more to his father's assistance than his own skill. "You will never hear me complain about being brought up with the name Dale Earnhardt, Jr., but don't for one minute believe that I had everything handed to me, though," he declared. "If you knew my father, you would never think that."

"You will never hear me complain about being brought up with the name Dale Earnhardt, Jr., but don't for one minute believe that I had everything handed to me, though."

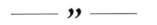

Earnhardt proved doubters wrong in 1999, winning his second consecutive Busch Series championship. His success in the 1999 campaign, which was highlighted by six race victories, made him one of only four drivers ever to win multiple Busch Series championships. It also vaulted him to a position as the most popular driver on the Busch circuit. "When you win the championship, people, as well as yourself, expect you to run like champions every year or the year after that," he said. "That little added pressure is there. . . . When you see the guys working hard at the shop and providing you the best race car you have, you want to put it up front."

Earnhardt's growing fame made him a popular interview with racing analysts and magazines. In these sessions, he was often asked about the experience of driving a car at 200 miles per hour. "In some ways, it's easy," he once said. "It's just simple physics. You have four tires on the car that connect to the asphalt or concrete. The key is to drive the car to the absolute edge of the tire's ability to grip that surface. It feels like you are on the verge of crashing at any moment when you're fighting a poor-handling car, but you just have to keep your foot in it and try to find that spot of ultimate speed.

"People ask if I can see things like fans in the grandstands when I'm driving that fast. I really can. When you run those speeds all the time, you just get used to them and everything seems to slow down. It must be like a professional baseball player who can almost see the stitching on a baseball that's been thrown at the plate at 95 miles per hour. The best moment for that was when I won my first Winston Cup race at Texas. On the last lap, I was trying to concentrate but I could see the fans going crazy, waving and yelling and taking hundreds of flash photographs."

Earnhardt also talked at length about the importance of his crew to his racing success. "It's so important that everyone is going in the same direction," he stressed. "If even one person is out of sync, you have almost no chance to win. When it does go all right, the feeling of victory is unbelievable. It is like a total release of energy and joy. It's unbelievable!"

At the Top of His Profession

Earnhardt's terrific performance in the Busch division stunned many observers — including his legendary father. "He surprised a lot of people, including me," Earnhardt Sr. admitted. "We knew he could drive a race car, but until you start winning on the racetrack and see how you react to the daily pressure, it's hard to know what you've got inside you."

Junior's Busch victories — and his famous name — made it a certainty that he would soon move up to the Winston Cup series. Sure enough, in September 1998 he signed a six-year sponsorship deal with Budweiser said to be worth as much as $10 million a year. Under the terms of the deal, Earnhardt ran five Winston Cup races in 1999 but spent most of his time on the Busch circuit. This arrangement enabled him to cruise to his second straight Busch Series championship. The deal then called for him to move up full-time to Winston Cup competition in 2000.

Earnhardt's deal with Budweiser, which also kept him driving with DEI, gave him his very first opportunity to race against his father in a NASCAR event. The most memorable of these encounters came in 1999, when Junior participated in his first handful of Winston Cup events. At a race in Michigan, the two Earnhardts found themselves pitted in a tense duel for victory over the last 50 laps. Earnhardt Sr. ultimately edged his son out to the checkered flag by .007 of a second, the closest finish in the history of the speedway. "That was one of the fondest memories of my career," Junior said afterward. "Something like that was not expected. I really had never expected to race him in my life, then to be able to race, me and him, one on one, with no one else in competition. . . . It was really nerve-wracking. . . . It came down to the last lap and it was pretty cool. To come as close as I

*Earnhard (8) racked up two victories in 2000, his first full season
of Winston Cup competition.*

did made me feel pretty good." More importantly, these sorts of shared experiences seemed to be bringing father and son closer together than ever before.

In 2000—Earnhardt's first full season of Winston Cup competition—he finished in the middle of the racing pack. He earned two victories in 34 starts and finished 16th in the season-ending point totals. The following year he moved up into the upper ranks of NASCAR drivers. In 36 starts, he won three races and claimed a total of nine top-five finishes to claim a number eight ranking in the season-ending standings. But it was hard for Earnhardt to enjoy these successes, as he spent the entire 2001 season grappling with a family tragedy that shook the world of NASCAR to its core.

Triumph and Tragedy at Daytona

The NASCAR racing season begins in February each year at Daytona Beach, Florida, with the Daytona 500, stock car racing's most prestigious event. During Earnhardt Sr.'s long and illustrious career, this race had become a source of enormous frustration to him. Even as he racked up win after win at other tracks around the country, a Daytona 500 victory eluded him. "Year after year after year you'd see my dad run second or blow his tire out or flip down the straightaway," recalled Junior. "Not many things ate that man's insides out, but losing this race over and over you could see that on his face." Finally, in 1998, Earnhardt Sr. took the checkered flag at the Daytona 500 in his 21st attempt.

As the 2001 Daytona 500 approached, Junior was looking forward to racing against his father on the storied track. When the race got underway on February 18, it was clear that Earnhardt Jr. had one of the fastest cars in the race. Showing steady nerves and sound strategy, he guided the car to a second place finish. But as his father was completing his final lap around the track, he smashed into a wall and was killed instantly by the impact.

The death of the "Intimidator," as Earnhardt Sr. was known to legions of NASCAR fans, stunned the racing community. His passing also rocked Junior and the rest of the Earnhardt family. "The weeks after Dad's death were a blur," Earnhardt Jr. recalled. "I was surrounded by people all of the time, but it was like being on a raft in the ocean: surrounded by water but unable to drink any of it. I missed my dad every moment."

One week after the tragedy at Daytona Raceway, Earnhardt Jr. returned to NASCAR competition at North Carolina Speedway. "The decision to go back to racing right away was one everyone at DEI agreed with," recalled Earnhardt. "It's what we, as racers, do, and it's where we felt closest to our friends. If I hadn't raced that first weekend, I would have felt so much more helpless and miserable. I really didn't want to be *anywhere* — but being at the track seemed like the best place." As the race progressed, Earnhardt suffered a scary crash that hushed the capacity crowd, but he walked away unharmed.

> **"**
>
> *"The weeks after Dad's death were a blur," Earnhardt Jr. recalled. "I was surrounded by people all of the time, but it was like being on a raft in the ocean: surrounded by water but unable to drink any of it. I missed my dad every moment."*
>
> **"**

A Momentous Victory at Daytona

On July 7, 2001, the NASCAR circuit returned to Daytona for the Pepsi 400. Earnhardt ran among the leaders for most of the race, but with six laps to go he was stuck behind five drivers. "I wanna win this one pretty bad," he radioed to his crew, then weaved past the leaders to take the checkered flag in dramatic fashion. He then spun his car around the same infield grass his father had dug up with his tires following his 1998 Daytona 500 triumph. "I felt like I was rescued from a deserted island," Earnhardt said afterward. "After that race I was just wide open, wanting to hug everybody. It really got me back to normal."

In 2001 Earnhardt's sister Kelley (left) began managing his business affairs.

Many other people were thrilled to see him win as well. The hordes of NASCAR fans who had followed Earnhardt Sr. for years screamed their approval, and Junior's own family and friends expressed delight with the victory. "I think for Dale Jr., he really, really leaned on his dad for his support and needed that 'You did a good job' out of him," said his sister Kelley. "When he won and did it on his own, so to speak, under the circumstances and all, it was very satisfying. I think it solidified that he can be his own person and be successful."

Adjusting to the Spotlight

The death of Earnhardt's father required Junior to take greater responsibility not only for his own career, but for DEI, his father's company. Teresa Earnhardt took the reins at DEI after the tragedy at Daytona, but Junior's new stature as the company's leading driver placed many new demands on his time.

His father's death also pushed Junior even more squarely into the publicity limelight. At times, Earnhardt struggled to deal with these changes. The demands on his time became so intense that Kelley quickly convinced her brother to let her guide his career and take care of the officework and administrative duties that were plaguing him. "I called Dale up and said, 'I need to work for you, and you need me to come work for you,'" she remembered. "It took him about three weeks. He always had the trust in me, he knows how I operate."

Dealing with the spotlight of fame, however, remained difficult for Earnhardt. Even prior to his father's death, many observers felt that Junior was seeking to stake out an identity of his own. Weary of being known only as Dale Earnhardt Sr.'s son, he sometimes seemed to go out of his way to say and do things that would generate controversy among NASCAR fans. For example, he gave profanity-laced, boastful interviews to *Rolling Stone* and *Playboy,* and he tweaked country-music loving NASCAR fans by expressing a preference for rap music. He even gave MTV's *Cribs* television show a tour of his home, which included a basement dance club (called "Club E") that was notorious for wild parties.

Despite these actions, the size of Earnhardt's following continued to grow. But many of these fans, ranging from starstruck youths to older fans that had watched his father race for years, refused to give him much peace and quiet. One NASCAR veteran told *Sporting News* that Earnhardt could not go anywhere in public without attracting a crowd. "Poor kid," the veteran said. "I don't even think his daddy went through this. He had legions of fans but not these kids that are after Junior."

Success and Maturity

Earnhardt's 2002 NASCAR season was filled with peaks and valleys. On the one hand, he won two races and finished the season with 11 top-five finishes in 36 starts. But he also endured several poor finishes due to mechanical failures and crashes. The results of these races nudged him out of a top-ten spot in the season-ending Winston Cup series standings. Instead, he finished 11th.

During the 2003 season, however, many observers detected a change in Earnhardt. Noting his closure of "Club E" and his newfound interest in nutrition and fitness training, they speculated that Junior was learning to adjust both to his fame and to the loss of his father. Ty Norris, executive vice president with DEI, told *Sporting News* that "he is more attentive to everything going on in his life. I think he's feeling more comfortable in his role as a superstar in the sport. . . . I think a lot of times Dale Jr. thought people gave him things because of his name. In the last two or three years, he has become comfortable with the role because he feels like he has earned it. And he has."

Earnhardt agreed that he had made some changes in his approach to life. "Earlier, I made a conscious effort to distance myself from Dad's image. It was kinda wearing me out, always makin' a statement, 'I'm not him.' Now it doesn't matter. I credit my father for giving me his name, and everything else. I didn't have the vision for all this — it's a headache, all this hype." He also confirmed that he was paying more attention to his fitness level. "I used to not even pay attention to my health," he said. "I'd eat what I wanted to eat, I went wherever I wanted to, raised hell, didn't sleep. But it takes away how quick-witted you are and how sharp you are in the race car."

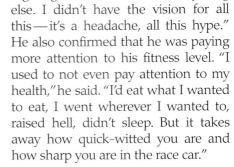

"Part of me always wants to stay under Dad's wing and be overshadowed by him in a way. . . . But there's a part of me that wants to break out and be my own man and get my own respect. Winning races like the Daytona 500 and doing the big things answers everybody's questions. Can you win championships? Can you win races? When you start to answer these questions, you become your own man."

Earnhardt finished the 2003 season with $6.8 million in earnings and a third-place finish in the Winston Cup standings. His banner season gave him nine career victories in Winston Cup competition and a career total of $20.4 million in earnings in 147 starts. He even made occasional appearances in the Busch Series, where he was dominant, winning five races in six starts during the 2002 and 2003 seasons.

In October 2003 Earnhardt announced an agreement to drive for DEI for the next five years. Around this same time, he learned that he had been voted NASCAR's Most Popular Driver in a nationwide poll conducted by the National Motorsports Press Association. In fact, he received more fan votes — 1.3 million — than the next nine drivers combined.

Winning the Daytona 500

On February 15, 2004, Earnhardt began the 2004 Nextel Cup (formerly the Winston Cup) season by winning the Daytona 500 on the same track where his father had been killed three years earlier. "When it came right

Earnhardt (8) passes Tony Stewart (20) on his way to taking the checkered flag at the 2004 Daytona 500.

down to it, all I could think about was, 'I can't believe I won!'" he said afterward. "The fans were going crazy. It was awesome. I wanted to just let it sink in, to have a minute for me."

The NASCAR community of fans and racing teams expressed almost universal happiness with Earnhardt's emotional triumph. Driver Tony Stewart, who finished second in the race, spoke for them all when he said afterward that "considering what this kid has gone through, losing his father here at the Daytona 500, it's nice to see him get his victory. I think his father's really proud today."

Earnhardt expressed both pride and humility about his victory. "I don't compete against my dad's fame," he said. "I want to do everything I can to honor him. Part of me always wants to stay under Dad's wing and be overshadowed by him in a way. Because he was taken so soon, it's almost like he still kind of takes care of me. But there's a part of me that wants to break out and be my own man and get my own respect. Winning races like the Daytona 500 and doing the big things answers everybody's questions. Can you win championships? Can you win races? When you start to answer these questions, you become your own man."

Earnhardt and his crew celebrate his emotional victory at the 2004 Daytona 500.

Midway through the 2004 campaign, Earnhardt was ranked 3rd in the Nextel Cup point standings. In late July he suffered burn injuries when his car burst into flames during competition at a raceway in Sonoma, California. But he was back in the driver's seat a week later, determined to make a run at the Nextel Cup Series Championship. Success in racing, he explained, "makes me feel like I'm putting in my part as far as carrying on the Earnhardt name. That's real important to me, that there's an Earnhardt out there to cheer for, doing good enough to cheer for. That makes me feel good. I just want to keep on racking up accomplishments so that when it's all done I can sit down and say I was a good race car driver and I made my daddy proud and I made my daddy's fans proud."

HOME AND FAMILY

Earnhardt lives in a secluded house near Lake Norman outside of Mooresville. "Mooresville is a great place to be," he said. "Mooresville is an old-school small town and a lot like Mayberry, North Carolina, the fictional town where *The Andy Griffith Show* took place."

Earnhardt hopes to get married before too much more time passes. "To be honest, I'm fired up about being married and having kids," he stated. "I want to have a son and enjoy what he does, whether it's racing or not. I just haven't found the girl yet."

"I just want to keep on racking up accomplishments so that when it's all done I can sit down and say I was a good race car driver and I made my daddy proud and I made my daddy's fans proud."

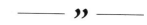

HOBBIES AND OTHER INTERESTS

"I like surfing the Internet, playing computer games, and hanging out at the mall," said Earnhardt. "What I am, I guess, is a normal guy who wants to stay that way. I like to drive around town, listening to music — everything from rap to alternative to Elvis or Merle Haggard. It might even be something like Fleetwood Mac that I remember my mother listening to on the car radio when I was little. I love music and I can't imagine my life without it."

Earnhardt also regularly works out in a regulation-sized boxing ring in his garage. He describes this activity as a challenging and enjoyable way of maintaining his physical fitness: "I guess I'm just growing up, like everybody else my age." He also lends his time to the Make-a-Wish Foundation, which provides fun experiences and opportunities for critically ill children. "We get so caught up in our work, [working with the Make-a-Wish Foundation] kind of gets you grounded," he explained. "It's a pleasure, really. [The kids] always seem to have a better attitude than I do."

WRITINGS

Driver #8, 2002 (with Jade Gurss)

HONORS AND AWARDS

Busch Series Championship: 1998, 1999
Most Popular Driver Award (National Motorsports Press Association):
    2003
Daytona 500 Championship: 2004

FURTHER READING

Books

Cothren, Larry. *Dale Earnhardt, Jr.: Standing Tall in the Shadow of a Legend,*
    2003
Cothren, Larry. *Earnhardt Racing Family Album,* 2004
Earnhardt, Dale, Jr., with Jade Gurss. *Driver #8,* 2002
Gigliotti, Jim. *Dale Earnhardt, Jr.: Tragedy and Triumph,* 2003 (juvenile)
Hembree, Michael. *Dale Earnhardt, Jr.: Out of the Shadow of Greatness,* 2004
Persinger, Kathy. *Dale Earnhardt, Jr.: Born to Race,* 2001 (juvenile)
Poole, David. *Dale Earnhardt, Jr.,* 2002 (juvenile)
Stewart, Mark. *Dale Earnhardt, Jr.: Driven by Destiny,* 2003 (juvenile)

Periodicals

Los Angeles Times, Feb. 18, 2000, p.D4
Men's Health, May 2004, p.96
Men's Journal, June 2003, p.60
Motor Trend, Nov. 2002, p.118
Newsweek, Apr. 15, 2002, p.46
Norfolk Virginian-Pilot, Feb. 16, 2002, p.C1
People Weekly, July 23, 2001, p.75; Mar. 8, 2004, p.71
Sporting News, Aug. 25, 2003, p.20; Oct. 13, 2003, p.45
Sports Illustrated, June 1, 1998, p.98; Dec. 22, 1999, p.78; Dec. 6, 2000, p.88;
    Feb. 28, 2001, p.60; July 1, 2002, p.61; Feb. 16, 2004, p.66; Feb. 23, 2004, p.48

Online Articles

http://www.nascar.com/2004/news/headlines/cup/08/07/dearnhardtjr_re-
    cover/index.html
    (*NASCAR.com,* "Dale Jr. Healing Wounds on Body, Within Team," Aug. 7,
    2004)

ADDRESS

Dale Earnhardt, Jr.
Club E Jr.
PO Box 5190
Concord, NC 28027

WORLD WIDE WEB SITES

http://www.daleearnhardtinc.com
http://www.dalejr.com
http://www.nascar.com

LeBron James 1984-

American Professional Basketball Player with the
Cleveland Cavaliers
2003-04 NBA Rookie of the Year

BIRTH

LeBron James was born on December 30, 1984, in Akron, Ohio.
His mother, Gloria James, was 16 and single at the time of his
birth. He is her only child. LeBron never knew his biological
father. For the first few years of LeBron's life, he and his mother lived with his maternal grandmother, Freda James, and his
two uncles, Terry and Curt. LeBron's uncles looked out for their
sister and tried to be father figures to him.

Another man in LeBron's young life was Eddie Jackson, who started dating his mother shortly after he was born and lived with his family for several years. Although Jackson and his mother never married and broke up when LeBron was still a child, LeBron continued to see Jackson over the years and still refers to him as "Dad."

YOUTH

LeBron James first held a basketball on Christmas morning in 1987—a few days before his third birthday. Part of a toy set that included a hoop, backboard, and stand, the ball was a gift from his mother and her then-boyfriend, Eddie Jackson. Jackson had been living with the James family at the invitation of LeBron's grandmother. Freda James was a kind and compassionate person, and she liked Jackson for his sweet, sensitive nature. She opened the door to him when he began dating her daughter and needed a place to stay.

Jackson and LeBron bonded very quickly and spent hours playing together. For example, Jackson indulged the child's enthusiasm for the staged antics of the World Wrestling Federation. He often wrestled with LeBron, who loved to assume the identity of Randy "Macho Man" Savage and other WWF stars. In fact, LeBrown often imitated Savage by yelling "I'm coming off the top rope!" and then leaping through the air to body-slam Jackson.

As soon as LeBron received his toy basketball set, however, he became as fascinated with the new game as he had been with WWF wrestling. "LeBron would be in his diaper, dunking all over that rim," recalled Terry James. Since the high-spirited boy kept toppling the hoop over, the adults kept raising the height of the basket. But the higher basket only inspired LeBron to show how high he could jump. "I kept raising it, and he kept dunking," his mother remembered. "All he would do is start back from the living room, run through the dining room, and he was still dunking the ball," added Jackson. "I was thinking, 'Man, this kid has some elevation for just being three years old.'"

Unfortunately, the family's happy Christmas of 1987 ended in sorrow. Later that day, LeBron's grandmother collapsed in the kitchen and died of a massive heart attack at the age of 42. The death of Freda James had a long-lasting effect on LeBron's life. His mother and uncles were unable to maintain the house, which had been deteriorating steadily for years. Within a few months, they were all forced to move out and support themselves. Gloria James, now 19, broke up with Jackson, moved into a public housing project in Akron, and began raising LeBron as a single mother.

Overcoming Poverty and Hardships

LeBron and his mother lived together in relative poverty for years, moving from apartment to apartment as Gloria James worked in a variety of jobs. When LeBron was five, they moved seven times over the course of a year. His unsettled home life affected his school work. In the fourth grade, for example, he missed 82 days of school out of 160. In search of some stability, he ended up spending part of the year living with the family of Frankie Walker, his basketball coach. "It changed my life," LeBron related. "The next year I had perfect attendance and a B average." While in the fifth and sixth grades, LeBron divided his time between his mother's house and the Walkers' home.

"We called ourselves the Fab Four," LeBron recalled. "We decided we'd all go to the same school together. We promised that nothing would break us up — girls, coaches, basketball. We'd hang together, no matter what."

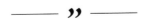

While some of his peers joined gangs or turned to drugs or crime, for the most part LeBron managed to stay out of trouble. "He's a good kid," his mother noted. "I never had to spank LeBron, not even once. When I tell him something, he listens." Eddie Jackson, however, had several brushes with the law. In 1991 he was sentenced to spend three years in prison for drug trafficking. He reentered the lives of LeBron and his mother after receiving parole in 1993. Jackson took a job as a full-time drug counselor and began providing financial support to Gloria James.

Meanwhile, LeBron's athletic ability and his love for the game of basketball grew by leaps and bounds. From the time he joined his first organized basketball league at the age of nine, he dominated other players with his unusual size and strength. "Even then, he was the biggest kid on the court," said one of his early coaches, Dru Joyce. "He was big, but he could handle the ball, and he had this uncanny ability to pass the ball."

LeBron soon hooked up with a group of friends who shared his love for basketball. He befriended Dru Joyce, Jr., the coach's son, and Sian Cotton. The three boys played together on a youth team called the Shooting Stars. Willie McGee, who played on an opposing team, eventually joined the Shooting Stars as well. LeBron, Dru, Sian, and Willie became inseparable friends and teammates. Their team won a total of more than 200 games, including several national league competitions. "We called ourselves the

Fab Four," LeBron recalled. "We decided we'd all go to the same school together. We promised that nothing would break us up — girls, coaches, basketball. We'd hang together, no matter what."

EDUCATION

Once James and the other members of the Fab Four completed eighth grade, they all decided to attend St. Vincent-St. Mary, a private Catholic school in Akron. The four freshmen ranked among the top eight players on the school's varsity basketball team. Their talent helped the Fighting Irish post a perfect 27-0 record during the 1999-2000 season and claim the Division III Ohio state championship. James played point guard and led his teammates by shooting 50 percent from the field and averaging 18 points and 8 rebounds per game. Although it was already clear that James had exceptional talent, head coach Keith Dambrot described the young star as a real team player. "If he wanted, LeBron could have scored 25 points a game, easy," he stated. "But he'd rather pass than shoot. That's why I think he can handle things and still fit in with the rest of the team."

In the Fab Four's sophomore year, James averaged 25 points and 7 rebounds a game as the Irish sailed through a 27-1 season. Their only loss was to Virginia's Oak Hill Academy, a top-ranked team that had dominated national competition in recent years.

Although James scored a game-high 33 points against the Oak Hill Warriors, he wept inconsolably as he walked off the court. "I know to this day, LeBron never got over that loss," said Fighting Irish assistant coach Steve Culp. "There are certain games that you will always keep with you as an athlete, games that you just don't forget. There is no doubt that the Oak Hill game his sophomore year hurt more than any other." But even though the loss snapped the Irish's 36-game winning streak, James and his teammates rebounded to claim another Ohio state championship.

During James's sophomore year, he also made his mark on the school gridiron. His decision to try out for the St. Vincent-St. Mary football team shocked his friends and basketball coaches, but he quickly proved that he belonged. His height and leaping ability helped him make the varsity squad as a wide receiver. He caught 42 passes — including 14 touchdown receptions — as a sophomore and was chosen team MVP on offense. James continued playing football for the Irish for the remainder of his high school career, even as he cemented his reputation as one of the top prep basketball players in the country.

James became a high school basketball sensation playing for the
St. Vincent-St. Mary Irish in Akron, Ohio.

Emerging as the Nation's Top High School Player

By age 16, James was being hailed by many observers as one of the best
basketball players—of any age—in the United States. Showcasing his talent at such high-profile, invitation-only basketball camps as the Nike All-
America camp and the Adidas ABCD camp, James dazzled talent scouts
with his passing ability, three-point shooting, and on-court vision. Many
noted that he seemed mature beyond his years and possessed the rare abil-

ity to make his teammates play better. Some called him a "basketball genius" and compared him to Hall of Fame players like Magic Johnson and Michael Jordan, his lifelong idol (James wore jersey number 23 in tribute to Jordan, who wore that number during his long career with the Chicago Bulls).

Upon returning to the court for his junior season in 2001-02, James averaged 28 points and 8 rebounds per game. The Irish fell short in their bid for a third straight state championship, but that disappointment did not diminish the roar of publicity that was rising around James. The hype surrounding the high school phenomenon reached a whole new level in February 2002, when the 17-year-old appeared on the cover of *Sports Illustrated*. The caption for the James cover photo proclaimed him as "The Chosen One," and sportswriter Grant Wahl wrote in the accompanying cover story that James already had the talent to play in the NBA. Wahl quoted Boston Celtics executive Danny Ainge as saying, "There are only four or five NBA players that I wouldn't trade to get him right now. If LeBron came out this year, I wouldn't even have to think about it. I'd take him Number One."

James received so much attention from NBA scouts and the media that he considered skipping his senior year of high school and making himself available for the NBA draft. But he knew that the move would defy an NBA rule requiring draft candidates to wait until after their high school class graduates to declare their availability. Rather than risk a court battle over his eligibility, he decided to return to St. Vincent-St. Mary and earn his diploma.

As a senior in 2002-03, James averaged 31 points, 10 rebounds, 5 assists, and 3 steals per game. His outstanding performance helped the Irish post a 25-1 record and win the Division III Ohio state championship for the third time since his freshman year. The Irish also defeated top-ranked Oak Hill Academy to claim the *USA Today* national high school championship. James graduated in the spring of 2003.

Attracting Crowds and Controversy

During his four years at St. Vincent-St. Mary, James amassed a total of 2,657 points, 892 rebounds, and 523 assists. He also became a national phenomenon. So many people wanted to see him play that the Fighting Irish no longer played their home games at the high school gym. Instead, St. Vincent-St. Mary home games were moved to the University of Akron's 5,100-seat arena to accommodate the crowds. In 2002-03, the Irish sold an amazing 1,750 season tickets. Average attendance at James's high school games was over 4,000 — almost double what the university generally drew for its men's basketball games. Some Fighting Irish games were even broadcast nationally by the cable-television sports channel ESPN.

The attention and publicity surrounding James's high school basketball career created some controversy. For example, many people became suspicious when Gloria James bought her son an $80,000 vehicle as an early graduation present. The special-edition Hummer featured three televisions, a DVD player, a PlayStation 2, and a custom "King James" leather interior. Critics questioned how Gloria James, who spent much of LeBron's childhood on welfare, could afford such extravagance. They accused LeBron of accepting gifts and loans based on his future marketability and NBA earnings.

The Ohio High School Athletic Association (OHSAA) conducted an investigation to determine whether the purchase broke its rule against amateur athletes "capitalizing on athletic fame by receiving money or gifts." The OHSAA ultimately found that Gloria James had taken out loans to buy the car and ruled the purchase acceptable. A short time later, however, the OHSAA suspended LeBron for two games for accepting gift jerseys from a Cleveland storeowner.

CAREER HIGHLIGHTS

NBA — The Cleveland Cavaliers

Shortly before he graduated from high school, James declared his availability for the NBA draft. His decision to skip college and turn professional did not surprise anyone, and few people doubted that the 6 foot, 7 inch, 230-pounder possessed the physical skills to succeed in the NBA. Still, many people criticized the NBA's policy of allowing players to join the pros straight out of high school. They claimed that teenagers like James were not mature enough to handle the attention and pressure of being an NBA star. They also argued that James would be better off getting a college education so that he would have a career to fall back on after his basketball days ended.

Despite such opinions, it was clear that James would be the first player selected in the 2003 NBA draft. The top choice ended up going to the Cleveland Cavaliers, a struggling franchise that had won only 17 out of 82 games the previous year. Cavaliers fans rejoiced when they learned that Cleveland received the top pick in the draft, because they knew that the team would select James, a virtual "hometown hero" since he had grown up in nearby Akron.

James soars for a dunk against the Philadelphia 76ers.

As the draft approached, James took the advice of Eddie Jackson and hired Alexandria Boone, a media consultant and friend, to handle his publicity. Boone hired Fred Nance, a Cleveland attorney, to help with contract negotiations. With the help of his advisors, James signed a three-year, $13-million contract with the Cavaliers. Even before he played in his first NBA game, James also arranged several large endorsement deals. For example, he signed a seven-year, $90-million contract with Nike that was widely considered to be the largest initial endorsement deal ever given to an athlete. He also negotiated more than $10 million in other, smaller deals.

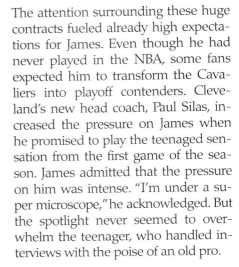

— " —

"LeBron James is really gifted," said scouting expert Marty Blake. "He's a player who comes around once every 20 years. He is a point guard in a power forward's body, and he's an amazing passer. It's really unusual. There's a lot of hype right now, but this is real."

— " —

The attention surrounding these huge contracts fueled already high expectations for James. Even though he had never played in the NBA, some fans expected him to transform the Cavaliers into playoff contenders. Cleveland's new head coach, Paul Silas, increased the pressure on James when he promised to play the teenaged sensation from the first game of the season. James admitted that the pressure on him was intense. "I'm under a super microscope," he acknowledged. But the spotlight never seemed to overwhelm the teenager, who handled interviews with the poise of an old pro.

Some analysts predicted that James would justify all the hype. "LeBron James is really gifted," said scouting expert Marty Blake. "He's a player who comes around once every 20 years. He is a point guard in a power forward's body, and he's an amazing passer. It's really unusual. There's a lot of hype right now, but this is real."

Other experts were more cautious in bestowing their praise. For example, Michael Jordan ranked James "toward the bottom" of the upper echelon of players in the NBA. "He has unbelievable potential, but he hasn't played against the competition consistently in college or the pros. He's played against high school kids who are probably under six feet [tall] and have the talent of sportswriters," Jordan continued. "Five years from now, if he takes on the dedication of being the best basketball player he can be and continues to improve and accepts challenges and does not get comfortable with what's been given to him, or what the expectations may be, he can definitely be a good pro."

NBA Rookie of the Year

As tip-off for the 2003-04 NBA season approached, James expressed quiet confidence that even at the professional level, he would continue to feel the same simple joy playing basketball that he had always felt. He seemed especially happy to be beginning his NBA career in his home state. "This is going to be great," he said. "My boys get to come watch me play, my family and all the Cavs fans. We're finally going to get more life in this city. I think what I'm going to do for this team is make us a family."

To the amazement of many observers, James managed to meet or even exceed the high expectations surrounding his NBA debut. James started 79 games for the Cavaliers

James (right) scorched the New Jersey Nets for a career-high 41 points on March 27, 2004.

and played a total of 3,122 minutes to rank ninth in the league in playing time for the 2003-04 season. He averaged an impressive 20.9 points, 5.5 rebounds, 5.9 assists, and 1.65 steals per game. James became only the third rookie in NBA history—joining Oscar Robertson and Michael Jordan—to average more than 20 points, 5 rebounds, and 5 assists per game in his first professional season. He led all first-year players in steals, ranked second in scoring, third in assists, and fifth in rebounds.

James's contributions helped the Cavaliers double its number of victories from the previous season and finish the year with a 35-47 record. Although the team finished below .500, they only missed the playoffs by one game. James's most outstanding performance came in a game against the New Jersey Nuggets on March 27, 2004. He scored 41 points to become the youngest player ever to score more than 40 points in a single game. James was named Eastern Conference Rookie of the Month every month of the season, receiving the honor six times in all. At the end of the season, he was named 2003-04 NBA Rookie of the Year.

Despite James's stellar rookie season, some critics still question whether the 19-year-old star will be mature enough to stay focused on the game.

They worry that the constant media attention and multi-million dollar product endorsement contracts could prove too much of a distraction for him. But Cavaliers Head Coach Paul Silas expressed confidence in his star point guard. Although James can be "very playful at times," Silas noted, "as far as basketball is concerned, there's no way he acts like he's only 18. He's much more mature." For his part, James claims that he is determined to improve his skills and help his team win. "What I care about is winning and making the playoffs," he stated. "I don't get caught up in all the attention and stuff, because I know I need to work on everything. Every aspect of my game needs improving."

"[Playing for Cleveland] is going to be great," James said. *"My boys get to come watch me play, my family and all the Cavs fans. We're finally going to get more life in this city. I think what I'm going to do for this team is make us a family."*

The 2004 Olympics

During the summer following his rookie NBA season, James became the youngest male basketball player ever to compete in the Olympics. The U.S. Men's Basketball Team entered the 2004 Games in Athens, Greece, as a heavy favorite. Since the U.S. Olympic Committee first decided to allow NBA players to represent the country in 1992, the American men had posted a 109-2 record against international competition and claimed three consecutive gold medals in men's basketball.

James joined a team of NBA stars that included Allen Iverson, Tim Duncan, and Carmelo Anthony. He was excited to be chosen to represent his country. "The Olympics are going to be a great opportunity," he stated. "I just feel we'll go over there and come home with a gold medal." Once the Olympic tournament began, however, he was disappointed by how little he played. Larry Brown, head coach of the American team, acknowledged that James found his greatly reduced role in the Games to be a "terrible adjustment." "The idea was to get young kids that would sit and learn and be the future of our Olympic team," Brown explained, "and it's been very hard for [him] to figure that out."

Although the American squad boasted many talented players, Team USA had trouble adjusting to international rules and failed to jell as a team. As a result, James and his teammates were upset by Argentina, Lithuania, and Puerto Rico during the Olympic tournament. The American men still made

James in action against Lithuania at the 2004 Summer Olympics.

it to the bronze medal game, where they faced Lithuania once again. In only 7 minutes of playing time, James scored 6 points and tallied 2 steals and 2 assists. Team USA won the game, 104-96, to claim the bronze medal.

Given the high expectations that had surrounded the U.S. men's basketball team, its third-place finish was widely viewed as a disappointment. Still, James said that he learned a great deal from the experience. "I just wanted to be on the Olympic team and have the experience," he noted. "Everything on the court I did not expect, but I think I'd do it again."

"My mother is my mother," James said. "But she also is my sister, my brother, my best friend, my uncle, my everything."

HOME AND FAMILY

LeBron James, who is single, lives in Akron, Ohio. He remains close to his mother, Gloria James. "My mother is my mother," James said. "But she also is my sister, my brother, my best friend, my uncle, my everything." James shows his devotion to his mother with a tattoo on his arm. She can often be seen in the stands at Cleveland Cavaliers games wearing a number 23 team jersey that says "LeBron's Mom" on the back.

HONORS AND AWARDS

Ohio Mr. Basketball (Associated Press): 2001-03
Gatorade Player of the Year: 2002-03
High School Boys Basketball Player of the Year (*Parade Magazine*): 2002-03
High School Boys Basketball Player of the Year (*USA Today*): 2002-03
McDonald's High School Basketball All-American: 2003
NBA Rookie of the Year: 2004
NBA All-Rookie First Team: 2004

FURTHER READING

Books

Morgan, David Lee. *The Rise of a Star: LeBron James,* 2003

Periodicals

Akron (Ohio) Beacon Journal, Nov. 26, 2000, p.D1; July 15, 2001, p.D1; Apr. 20, 2004

Cleveland Plain Dealer, Feb. 16, 2003, p.A1; Mar. 13, 2003, p.B1
Cleveland Scene, Jan. 17, 2002
Ebony, June 2003, p.174; Jan. 2004, p.124
ESPN Magazine, Nov. 10, 2003, p.58
Los Angeles Times, Jan. 4, 2003, p.D1; Oct. 16, 2003, p.D1
New York Times, Feb. 1, 2003, p.D1
St. Louis Post-Dispatch, Apr. 4, 2004, p.D10
Slam, Aug. 2003, p.85
Sports Illustrated, Feb. 18, 2002, p.62; Oct. 27, 2003, p.68; Mar. 15, 2004, p.54
USA Today, Nov. 28, 2001, p.C3; May 8, 2002, p.C7; Dec. 11, 2002, p.A1; Dec. 13, 2002, p.C3

Online Articles

http://sports.espn.go.com
  (ESPN.com, "Matching the Hype," Apr. 15, 2004)

Online Databases

Biography Resource Center Online, 2003

ADDRESS

LeBron James
Cleveland Cavaliers
Gund Arena Company
One Center Court
Cleveland, OH 44115-4001

WORLD WIDE WEB SITES

http://www.lebronjames.com
http://www.nba.com/cavaliers
http://www.cleveland.com/lebron
http://www.nbadraft.net/profiles/lebronjames.htm

Carly Patterson 1988-
American Gymnast
Gold Medalist in the Women's Individual All-Around
at the 2004 Olympic Games

BIRTH

Carly Rae Patterson was born on February 4, 1988, in Baton Rouge, Louisiana. Her father, Ricky Patterson, works in the automobile industry, and her mother, Natalie Patterson, is a registered nurse. She has a younger sister, Jordan, who was born in 1990. Her parents divorced around 2001, and her father later remarried.

YOUTH

Carly showed a talent for gymnastics from an early age. "I was flipping around the house by two years old," she remembered. She could often be found bouncing on the furniture and off the walls, and she taught herself to do cartwheels and handsprings before she reached school age. In 1994, when Carly was six, she attended an older cousin's birthday party at a local gymnastics facility. The gym owner, former Olympian Johnny Moyal, immediately recognized her natural ability and encouraged her parents to enroll her in lessons. "She was very talented physically, a great athlete," he recalled. "This little girl looked like she was something special."

Carly's mother worried that she was too young to start formal gymnastics training. But once Carly was exposed to the sport, there was no stopping her. "After the party, she had this incredible drive," Natalie Patterson remembered. "She came home and was determined to learn a flip-flop [back handspring], and I thought we're either going to get her into gymnastics or she's going to get a broken neck."

Carly soon enrolled in classes at Elite Gymnastics in Baton Rouge. Her skills allowed her to move up quickly through the levels of amateur competition. USA Gymnastics divides gymnasts into 11 classifications according to skill level. There are numbered divisions from 1 to 10, with 10 being the

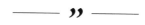

Carly competed in her first gymnastics meet just four months after she began training and was thrilled to finish 13th. "I was just so excited to compete and get a ribbon," she said.

highest, and an upper division called elite. The elite division includes junior and senior athletes competing at the national and international levels. Gymnasts who compete in the Olympics are classified as senior international elite. When Carly first entered competitive gymnastics, her skills qualified her for Level 4. She competed in her first gymnastics meet just four months after she began training and was thrilled to finish 13th. "I was just so excited to compete and get a ribbon," she said.

During her five years at Elite Gymnastics, Carly progressed from Level 4 to Level 10. She reached Level 8 at the age of 9, and attained Level 10 by the time she was 11. In 1999 she earned the title of Louisiana Level 10 State Champion. A short time later her father received a job transfer and the family moved to Texas. For the next year Carly trained at Brown's Gymnastics in Houston. Then her father was transferred again and the family moved to Allen, Texas, near Dallas. This move gave Carly the opportunity to train at one of the best facilities in the United States — the World Olympic Gymnastics Academy (WOGA) in nearby Plano.

At WOGA Carly began working with a new coach, Evgeny Marchenko. A native of the former Soviet republic of Kazakhstan, Marchenko was a five-time world champion in sports acrobatics, which is similar to gymnastics. He immediately appreciated Carly's athletic ability, determination, and grace under pressure. "As soon as she came to us years ago, I thought, She's the one, my first Olympic champion," he related. "From the start she was able to perform with all the cameras and people and pressure. She's a very competitive girl. After she makes a mistake, she fights back."

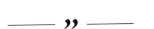

> "I just kept throwing skills out there, but without ever being taught the right technique — like how to point my toes or keep my knees straight," Carly admitted. "I had bad form. Bad everything. And it took a long time before I started to get better."

But the new coach also told Carly that she needed to improve her fundamentals and correct some bad habits if she hoped to succeed as an elite gymnast. "I just kept throwing skills out there, but without ever being taught the right technique — like how to point my toes or keep my knees straight," Carly admitted. "I had bad form. Bad everything. And it took a long time before I started to get better."

EDUCATION

When her family first moved to Allen, Carly attended the public schools there. As her gymnastics training required more and more of her time, however, she transferred from Allen High School to Spring Creek Academy in Plano. This private school is located near WOGA and offers flexible schedules for young athletes in training. During the school year, Carly's typical schedule involves spending three hours at the gym in the morning, followed by five 30-minute school classes and a study hall in the afternoon, then three more hours at the gym in the evening.

Despite the demands of her training, Carly is a straight-A student who entered the 11th grade in the fall of 2004. Her favorite classes are Spanish and child development. Once her gymnastics career is over, she plans to attend college and study dental hygiene. She eventually hopes to become a dentist or an orthodontist. "I have a thing for straight, white teeth," she explained. "I don't know why I've been so interested in teeth, but that's what I've wanted to do for my whole life. It's kind of weird, but I like it."

CAREER HIGHLIGHTS

Joining the Ranks of Elite Gymnasts

In 2000—shortly after her family moved to Texas—Patterson moved up to the junior elite level in gymnastics. She soon proved that she deserved to be ranked among the top gymnasts in the United States by placing first in the balance beam at the U.S. Classic. The balance beam is one of five different events featured in women's gymnastics competitions. The other events are the uneven parallel bars, the vault, the floor exercise, and the all-around, in which competitors' scores for the other four events are combined. Patterson's performance at the U.S. Classic qualified her to compete in the junior division at the U.S. National Championships. In this meet she captured a silver medal in the balance beam and placed fourth in the all-around. At her first international gymnastics meet—the 2000 Top Gym Tournament in Belgium—Patterson earned a silver medal in the all-around and a bronze on the balance beam.

The next year was Patterson's first full competitive season at WOGA. She continued to perform well at national meets, moving up to third place in the all-around at the U.S. Junior National Championships. She also represented the United States at international meets in Australia and China. The highlight of her season came at the American Team Cup, where she introduced a distinctive dismount from the balance beam that came to be known as the "Patterson." She described her signature dismount as a "round-off, flip-flop, double Arabian." In other words, she performed a round-off and back-handspring on the beam, then launched herself off the end and did two front somersaults before landing on the floor. "It's a very risky trick with a blind landing," Marchenko noted. "It's pretty spectacular." The debut of the "Patterson" helped her win the all-around gold medal in the junior division at the American Team Cup.

In 2002—her last year at the junior elite level—Patterson rarely finished out of the top three in all-around competition. She easily won the U.S. Junior National Championship, and she performed well at a number of international meets in North and South America. Upon turning 15 years old in 2003, Patterson became eligible to compete at the highest level of gymnastics—senior international elite. She claimed her first senior all-around title at the Visa American Cup, defeating two apparatus world champions (Americans Courtney Kupets on uneven parallel bars and Ashley Postell on balance beam) and a double gold medalist from the 2000 Olympic Games

By her mid-teens, Patterson ranked among the top gymnasts in the United States.

(Russian Elena Zamolodchikova) in the process. Unfortunately, Patterson suffered a stress fracture in her elbow that prevented her from competing in the U.S. Classic and U.S. National Championships later that year.

Facing Adversity at the 2003 World Championships

Patterson took several weeks off from training in order to give her elbow time to heal. "My arm feels great and I think it's getting better and better every day," she said afterward. Despite missing the U.S. National Championships, she was selected to represent the United States at the 2003 World Gymnastics Championships. At 15, Patterson was the youngest member of the American team. She was thrilled to make her international debut as a senior gymnast at such a prestigious competition. "Workouts are going really well, I'm getting in shape, and I think I'm ready," she declared. "I'm maybe a little nervous, but I'm mostly excited. This will definitely be the biggest meet that I've ever competed in."

The first part of the World Championships was the team competition. Each of the 70 participating nations selected three gymnasts to compete in each of the four events. Their scores were combined to form a team score, and the team with the highest total score won the team all-around championship. The order in which the national teams finished at the 2003 World Championships was important because only the top 12 teams would earn spots in the 2004 Olympic Games. Patterson and her teammates performed extremely well in the competition. They became the first U.S. team ever to win a World Championship gold medal in the team all-around.

While helping the American team take the world title, however, Patterson reinjured her elbow. She tried applying ice, using electrical stimulation, and massaging it, but nothing seemed to help. "It swelled up and was really throbbing," she recalled. "I didn't want to find out what was wrong because I knew they'd tell me not to compete. So I just tried to block it out and keep pushing myself."

"[My elbow] swelled up and was really throbbing," Patterson recalled. "I didn't want to find out what was wrong because I knew they'd tell me not to compete. So I just tried to block it out and keep pushing myself."

Despite the fact that she could not straighten her arm completely, Patterson continued competing for two more days in the individual all-around competition. She turned in a gutsy performance and ended up finishing second to the defending world champion, Svetlana Khorkina of Russia, by .188 of a point. (Judges award scores for each routine based on its degree of difficulty and the gymnast's performance. The maximum number of points for any one event is 10.0.) Once the competition ended, Patterson finally submitted to a medical evaluation of her elbow. In addition to aggravating the previous injury, she had suffered another fracture and damaged a ligament. She needed surgery to repair the joint, followed by three months of rest. "I really admire her toughness, her motivation, and her discipline," her coach said afterward. "She pushes herself very hard."

After winning the all-around silver medal at the World Championships, Patterson announced that she was turning professional. Although she would

Patterson soars above the balance beam at the U.S. gymnastics trials for the 2004 Summer Olympics.

still be allowed to compete in the Olympics, her decision meant that she would lose her college eligibility. "At that point, Carly decided when she went to college she probably wouldn't want to do gymnastics," her mother explained. As a professional gymnast, Patterson began collecting prize money for performing in tours and winning titles. She also signed endorsement contracts with such major corporations as Visa, AT&T Wireless, and McDonald's.

Coming Back for the 2004 National Championships

Patterson launched her comeback from the elbow injury in dramatic fashion in February 2004 at the Visa American Cup. She won all four events to successfully defend her all-around title. "Carly's performance was absolutely outstanding," said U.S. Olympic Gymnastics Team Coach Marta Karolyi. "She proved again she is one of our greatest competitors."

Patterson's next major test came at the 2004 U.S. National Championships in May. She found herself locked in a thrilling duel with Courtney Kupets for the all-around title. Kupets led by .05 after two rotations. Patterson took the lead with a powerful floor exercise that scored 9.8. In her final event, however, she performed a mediocre vault and opened the door for Kupets. Kupets entered her final apparatus—the uneven parallel bars— needing to score a 9.6 to tie Patterson for the lead, and her routine earned exactly that. The two gymnasts shared the all-around title. "I definitely don't wish upon anyone to screw up," Patterson noted. "It's really cool that we tied because I think we're both really great gymnasts."

The top 12 gymnasts from the National Championships moved on to the U.S. Olympic Trials three weeks later. The two top finishers at the trials would earn automatic berths on the American team that would compete in the 2004 Games in Athens, Greece. The remaining athletes would get one more chance to win one of the six coveted spots on the team at the Olympic selection camp in July. The final roster for the U.S. Olympic Team, which would also include three alternates, would be chosen by Marta Karolyi and a selection committee.

As the co-National Champion, Patterson entered the Olympic Trials determined to earn one of the guaranteed spots on the Olympic team. Unfortunately, she fell off of the balance beam during both of her performances and slipped to third place in the final standings. But she remained confident that she could overcome her poor showing. "I know what I did wrong—it was one of those fluke things—and I'm going back into the gym and I'm going to fix it," she stated. "She was possibly over cautious," her coach added. "When she falls, she falls. Her routines are very stable.

Patterson's floor routine in the all-around finals at the 2004 Olympics helped lift her to a gold medal.

She's very calm and cool. She never gave up. Her spirit was not broken, not damaged."

Patterson came back from her disappointing performance at the Olympic Trials to dominate the Olympic selection camp. She earned the highest single score awarded at the camp—a 9.9 on the floor exercise—on her way to claiming the highest all-around total for both days of competition. She thus won the right to represent the United States at the 2004 Olympic Games. She was joined on the American team by Mohini Bhardwaj, Annia Hatch, Terin Humphrey, Courtney Kupets, and Courtney McCool.

High Expectations

The American team entered the Athens Games as one of the favorites to win the gold medal. The United States boasted a deep talent pool in gymnastics, thanks in part to the success of the "Magnificent Seven" at the

1996 Olympic Games in Atlanta, Georgia. Led by Shannon Miller, Kerri Strug, Dominique Dawes, and Dominique Moceanu, the American women won the team gold medal in dramatic fashion that year. Some experts credited their performance with inspiring a whole new generation of American girls to enter the sport of gymnastics—including Patterson and her teammates.

Of all the talented gymnasts on the U.S. Olympic team, Patterson was the one singled out by many experts as a possible breakout star. Former gold medalist Nadia Comaneci, for example, said, "I'm really excited to see what Carly is going to do. I really think she's the girl with the potential to do something big." Another former Olympic champion, Mary Lou Retton, gave Patterson a poster with the inscription, "I saw you win silver at the worlds, but I'll see the gold on you in Athens." Mark Starr of *Newsweek* argued that Patterson combined the best traits of the stars of the 1996 team. "She has the skill set of Miller, the pizzazz of Dawes, the power of Moceanu, and the toughness of Strug," he wrote.

Patterson appreciated the kind words, but she tried to ignore the hype in order to concentrate on preparing for the Games. "I guess there can be high expectations and pressure, but I don't listen to it," she stated. "It doesn't bother me at all. There are a lot of other distractions out there. I just try to focus on my training."

> **"**
>
> *"I guess there can be high expectations and pressure, but I don't listen to it," Patterson stated. "It doesn't bother me at all. There are a lot of other distractions out there. I just try to focus on my training."*
>
> **"**

As the Olympic team competition approached, the U.S. coaches announced that Patterson would be the only American athlete to compete in all four events. Her favorite event—and the one for which she was best known—was the balance beam. Although her routine had a high degree of difficulty, she often seemed weightless as she flipped across the beam. "She has a very powerful body and legs," Marchenko explained, "but when she lands on the bar it's absolutely soundless." Patterson also performed a powerful floor exercise routine set to the song "Zoot Suit Riot" by the band Big Bad Voodoo Daddy. She added a high-energy routine on the uneven parallel bars that featured several dangerous release moves. Vault was typically her weakest event, where she admitted that "old, bad habits" sometimes created flaws in her technique.

As the Olympic team competition got underway, Patterson led off for the United States on vault and uneven parallel bars. Unfortunately, she turned in mediocre performances that ended up hurting the team. But she came back strong as the final performer in both balance beam and floor exercise. In the end, the American team finished second to the defending Olympic champions from Romania by a score of 114.283 to 113.584. Given the high expectations that had surrounded the U.S. women, some viewed the silver medal as a disappointment. But others pointed out that it was a vast improvement over the 2000 Games, when the American gymnasts failed to earn a single medal.

Golden Days

The next portion of the Olympic gymnastics competition was the individual all-around, which is widely considered to be the most prestigious event in the sport. Among the Americans, only Patterson and Kupets earned high enough scores in the preliminary round and team competition to qualify for the all-around final. Patterson's first rotation was her weakest event, the vault, and she got off to a rough start. Although she completed her rotations in the air, she landed outside the boundary lines for an automatic .2 deduction from her score. The 9.375 points she received put her in eighth place after the first round of competition. But Patterson realized that she still had a chance for a medal when her chief rival, World Champion Svetlana Khorkina of Russia, only earned a 9.462 on the vault. "I was a little crooked on my vault," Patterson acknowledged. "But I knew that if I could hit the best routines on my other routines I would have a chance."

In the second rotation of the individual all-around, Patterson posted a 9.575 on the uneven parallel bars and moved into fourth place. She followed up with a solid performance on the balance beam, earning 9.725 points. In contrast, Khorkina faltered on her beam routine and visibly struggled to regain her balance. The judges awarded her only 9.462 points, which allowed Patterson to take over the lead.

The two athletes' fight for the gold medal came down to the final rotation — the floor exercise. Khorkina's routine, which featured graceful and balletic sequences but had a relatively low degree of difficulty, earned a 9.562. Patterson, who was the final gymnast to perform, only needed a score of 9.537 in order to win the all-around gold medal. Rather than playing it safe, however, she turned in a powerful and athletic routine with a high degree of difficulty. Her score of 9.712 allowed her to defeat Khorkina by .176 of a point, 38.387 to 38.211. Patterson thus became the first American Olympic all-around champion in 20 years — since Mary Lou

Patterson and coach Evgeny Marchenko wave to the crowd after learning that she won the gold medal in the women's gymnastics individual all-around final.

Retton in 1984—and the first U.S. woman ever to win an all-around title in a fully attended Olympic Games (the Soviet Union and several other countries boycotted the 1984 Games). Khorkina took the silver medal, and Zhang Nan of China won the bronze.

When Patterson's final score appeared on the scoreboard, she ran to her coach and jumped into his arms. "I said to her, 'You are the Olympic champion,' and she started crying," Marchenko recalled. "And then so did I." After regaining her composure, Patterson acknowledged the cheers of the crowd. At the medalists' press conference afterward, the 16-year-old American gushed, "I've been dreaming about this my whole life." Many others were thrilled by Patterson's accomplishment as well. "Wow. Beautiful. That was fantastic," said legendary gymnastics coach Bela Karolyi. "It is 1984 again—silver for the team, and an all-around gold medal. How many years have we waited? Twenty years? Golly, can you believe it?"

―――― **"** ――――

"When there is a really big crowd, I want to perform my best. That helps me. I don't know why. Some people are nervous in front of big crowds. But I like it better. I can get better under pressure."

―――― **"** ――――

As he beamed over Patterson's triumph, Karolyi also predicted that her gold medal performance would inspire a new generation of American girls to enter the sport of gymnastics. "There is an army coming behind her," he said. "I guarantee you that now millions of girls are going to watch the Olympics and say, 'I want to be the next Carly Patterson.'"

A few days after her triumph in the all-around, Patterson added a silver medal for balance beam in the individual event finals. Her score of 9.775 ranked a close second behind the 9.787 earned by gold medalist Catalina Ponor of Romania. Afterward, Patterson claimed that the pressure of the Olympics actually aided her performance. "It gives me a lot of adrenaline and confidence," she stated. "When there is a really big crowd, I want to perform my best. That helps me. I don't know why. Some people are nervous in front of big crowds. But I like it better. I can get better under pressure."

HOME AND FAMILY

Patterson lives in Allen, Texas, with her mother and younger sister. She has two cats, Beijing and Java, and hopes to get a dog someday. After her parents' divorce, her father moved back to Louisiana and remarried. She talks to her dad on the telephone a couple of times each week and sees him whenever she can.

HOBBIES AND OTHER INTERESTS

In addition to spending between 35 and 40 hours per week in the gym, Patterson follows a strict diet consisting of chicken, fish, vegetables, yogurt, salad, and granola. Although her lifestyle involves some sacrifices, she claims that it is worth it. "It's tough sometimes because you miss out on attending a regular school, going out on weekends, sleeping in, or having more of a normal life. But that's what you give up to become a world-class gymnast," she acknowledged. "I'll have the rest of my life to do all those other things. . . . I've had the chance to travel the world and see things that most people don't get to see in their whole life. I'm happy with my accomplishments in gymnastics."

In her limited spare time, Patterson enjoys swimming in her backyard pool, riding her bike, messaging friends on her computer, going shopping, and watching movies. She recently got her driver's license and loves driving — even if her usual destination is the gym.

HONORS AND AWARDS

U.S. Junior National Gymnastics Championship, Individual All-Around: bronze, 2001; gold, 2002
World Gymnastics Championship, Team Competition: gold, 2003
World Gymnastics Championship, Individual All-Around: silver, 2003
Visa American Cup, Individual All-Around: gold, 2003; gold, 2004
Olympic Women's Gymnastics, Team Competition: silver, 2004
Olympic Women's Gymnastics, Individual All-Around: gold, 2004
Olympic Women's Gymnastics, Balance Beam: silver, 2004

FURTHER READING

Books

Valentine, Susan. *Carly Patterson: Olympic Idol,* 2004

Periodicals

Christian Science Monitor, June 2, 2004, p.15
Houston Chronicle, Aug. 20, 2004, p.1
Los Angeles Daily News, Aug. 23, 2003, p.S1

New York Times, June 6, 2004, p.SP9; Aug. 20, 2004, p.D1
Newark (N.J.) Star-Ledger, June 25, 2004, p.49
Newsweek, Aug. 16, 2004, p.45
Sports Illustrated, Aug. 30, 2004, p.48
Time, Aug. 30, 2004, p.55
USA Today, June 2, 2004, p.C1; June 7, 2004, p.C7

ADDRESS

Carly Patterson
USA Gymnastics
Pan American Plaza
201 South Capitol Avenue
Suite 300
Indianapolis, IN 46225

WORLD WIDE WEB SITES

http://www.carlypatterson.com
http://www.usa-gymnastics.org
http://www.usolympicteam.com
http://www.nbcolympics.com/carlypatterson

Albert Pujols 1980-

Dominican-Born American Professional Baseball
Player with the St. Louis Cardinals
National League Rookie of the Year in 2001 and
National League Batting Champion in 2003

BIRTH

Jose Alberto Pujols (pronounced *POO-holes*), known as Albert,
was born on January 16, 1980, in Santo Domingo, Dominican
Republic. The Dominican Republic is an island nation in the
Caribbean Sea, and Santo Domingo is its capital city. Albert's
mother left the family when he was very young. His father,

Bienvenido Pujols, traveled frequently in search of work. As a result, Albert was raised primarily by his paternal grandmother, America Pujols, along with his father's ten brothers and sisters. An only child, Albert came to view his older aunts and uncles as siblings. He moved to the United States with his family in 1996, at the age of 16, and became an American citizen a short time later.

YOUTH

Like many boys in the Dominican Republic, Albert loved baseball. He started playing at a young age and always dreamed of making it to the major leagues. His father was a good amateur pitcher, and young Albert enjoyed attending his local league games. "I think I learned more about baseball just playing all the time when I was young and watching how people approached things, watching my brothers and my dad and just trying to do the same things they did," he stated. He also watched American Major League Baseball on television whenever he had the opportunity. "I never chose one team as my favorite," he noted. "I always watched Sammy [Sosa] and [Raul] Mondesi and all the Latino players."

> *"No one ever told me I couldn't be a big-league ballplayer. They told me to keep working hard, that anyone who got there didn't get there easy."*

In the mid-1990s several of Albert's family members left the Dominican Republic in search of a better life in the United States. Albert and his father and grandmother joined them in 1996, when they immigrated to New York City. Within a month of their arrival, however, Albert witnessed a murder on his way to the grocery store. This incident convinced his family to find a different place to live. They ended up settling in Independence, Missouri, where they joined a community of about 2,000 Dominican immigrants.

At first the Pujols family was poor and struggled to adjust to life in the United States. But Albert's aunts and uncles gradually found jobs and became self-sufficient. His grandmother remained a guiding force at the center of the family who made sure that Albert and the others were well cared for. "She gave me everything I needed," he recalled. "She supported me 100 percent. How they treated me and took care of me, that's where I learned everything. And no one ever told me I couldn't be a big-league ballplayer. They told me to keep working hard, that anyone who got there didn't get there easy."

EDUCATION

After completing his early education in Santo Domingo, Pujols entered Fort Osage High School in Independence as a sophomore in the fall of 1996. He spoke only Spanish at the time, and the language barrier initially created problems for him at school. But he worked intensively with a tutor and became conversant in English within a year. In the spring of 1997 Pujols tried out for the Fort Osage varsity baseball team. Everyone who witnessed his tryout realized immediately that he possessed incredible talent. "Every time he swung, the bat was just going crack, crack, crack," recalled his high school coach, Dave Fry. "I looked at my coaches and said, 'What do we have here?' The more I watched him, I felt like the baseball gods had smiled down on me."

Pujols posted a batting average above .500 that year and hit 11 home runs to earn all-state honors. As a junior in 1998 he posted a .600 average with 8 home runs in just 33 at-bats. He also walked 55 times, because opposing teams were reluctant to give him any good pitches to hit (for statistical purposes, walks do not count as at-bats). Pujols led Fort Osage to the state baseball championship that year while earning all-state honors for the second time. Missouri baseball fans still talk about some of the monster home runs Pujols hit in high school, including a 450-footer that landed on top of a tall building located well beyond the left-field fence of an opponent's field.

Pujols chose to graduate from high school early in January 1999. Since opposing high school teams refused to pitch to him, he felt he could receive a better evaluation from professional baseball scouts by foregoing his senior season and moving on to college baseball. Eager to remain close to home, Pujols accepted a baseball scholarship to attend Maple Woods Community College in Kansas City. That spring, he hit a grand slam and turned an unassisted triple play at shortstop in his first junior college game. He went on to bat .461 with 22 home runs and 80 runs batted in (RBIs) for Maple Woods. Pujols left college after one semester in order to pursue his dream of playing major league baseball.

CAREER HIGHLIGHTS

Rocketing through the Minor Leagues

On the strength of his single college season, the St. Louis Cardinals selected Pujols in the 13th round of the 1999 Major League Baseball draft. At first he was so upset about his low draft position that he considered giving up baseball. "It did bother me. I won't lie. I was disappointed," he acknowledged. "One time, I thought I should quit baseball. But I prayed about it. God blessed me and gave me the chance. I decided I didn't care too much about where I got drafted. I knew if I was good enough, I would make it to the big leagues in three or four years."

Pujols signed a contract for $10,000 and entered the Cardinals' minor league system in the spring of 2000. He spent most of the season with the Class A Peoria Chiefs of the Midwest League, where he batted .314 with 19 home runs and 96 RBIs and was named the league's most valuable player (MVP). His strong performance earned him a promotion to the Class AA Potomac Cannons, but he did not remain there long before being promoted again. "He hit the ball harder and more often than anyone I had ever seen," said Bo Hart, one of his Cannons teammates. "Anytime he made an out, it just seemed that someone accidentally was there to catch the ball."

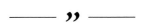

"I decided I didn't care too much about where I got drafted. I knew if I was good enough, I would make it to the big leagues in three or four years."

In the fall of 2000 Pujols was invited to join the Cardinals' Class AAA team in Memphis, Tennessee, for the Pacific Coast League playoffs. In just 7 games at that level, he batted .367 with 2 home runs and was named the playoffs MVP. Pujols's accomplishments in the minor leagues impressed the Cardinals' coaches, who invited him to join the big-league team for spring training in February 2001. The coaches believed that Pujols might have a future with the team as a third baseman, so they wanted to give him some exposure to the major league atmosphere.

The Cardinals' coaching staff did not intend to give Pujols a permanent slot on the major league roster. St. Louis had won the National League Central Division championship the year before, so the club was not in desperate need of new blood. Their intention was simply to give Pujols a taste of the big leagues, then send him back to Class AAA to develop his skills for another year or two. As spring training progressed, however, Pujols played so well that the Cardinals had no choice but to keep him on the major league roster. "Each week when we had our cut meetings, there we were, figuring he had to go back to the minors at some point, and each week he kept impressing us more and more," recalled Cardinals General Manager Walt Jocketty. "It got to the final week and we just said, 'Look, we're really a better club with him,' the way he was playing."

Pujols, shown here being mobbed by teammates after hitting one of his many clutch home runs, was the National League Rookie of the Year in 2001.

The final obstacle involved finding a spot for Pujols on the starting roster, because the coaches wanted the young player to see action every day in order to speed his development. By chance, a spot opened up when starting outfielder Bobby Bonilla suffered a hamstring injury shortly before the start of the season. "I'm glad things worked out the way they did, because he had just as good a spring as anybody on the team, if not the best spring," Bonilla stated. "He's going to do a lot more in this game, because his upside is huge. The most impressive thing about him is how he's been able to keep things on an even keel."

2001 National League Rookie of the Year

Pujols made his major league debut on April 2, 2001, and quickly established himself as a vital member of the St. Louis lineup. In fact, he became the first Cardinals rookie ever to hit a home run in the team's home opener. Pujols surprised many observers by ranking among the National League leaders in several offensive categories for much of the season. His performance at the plate remained consistent even as the Cards struggled to find a place for him in the field. In fact, Pujols played in four different defensive positions — first base, third base, left field, and right field — as the season progressed. He claimed that shuffling around from infield to outfield did not bother him. "I want to be in the lineup every day," he explained. "Playing anywhere is better than playing the bench."

Pujols also gained a reputation as one of the hardest-working members of his team. He always spent extra time at the ballpark taking batting and fielding practice, and he made a point of seeking the advice of coaches and veteran players. "There is nobody out there who can tell me they know all about everything in baseball," he noted. "You can't go higher than this level. So I have a lot I can learn from these guys. I pay attention to everything they do. This is where you try to stay for 10, 15, 20 years. They have the experience, and I'm trying to get this experience from them."

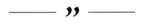

"I'm not trying to have a great year as a rookie setting records," Pujols said. "I am trying to get my baseball team into the playoffs and World Series. That is the only record that I want."

As the season unfolded, Pujols emerged as the clear leader for National League Rookie of the Year honors. In addition, he was named to the All-Star team in July. Despite his outstanding performance, Pujols still remained focused on helping his team. "I'm not trying to have a great year as a rookie setting records," he said. "I am trying to get my baseball team into the playoffs and World Series. That is the only record that I want." Pujols provided the spark that helped the Cardinals successfully defend their Central Division championship that year with a 93-69 record. But St. Louis was defeated in the division series 3-2 by the eventual World Series champion Arizona Diamondbacks.

Still, Pujols posted one of the best rookie seasons in major league history, as he came close to setting all-time rookie records for home runs, RBIs, doubles, extra-base hits, and slugging percentage. He batted .329 with 37 home runs, while walking 69 times and striking out only 93 times. He finished fifth in the National League in RBIs (with 130), hits (194), and doubles (47), and sixth in batting average and extra-base hits (88). As he received his Rookie of the Year award, Pujols was matter-of-fact about his performance. "I'm not surprised at all," he stated. "I've played baseball since I was five years old, and it was always my dream to be in the major leagues. I've worked hard to get here, and I'm working hard to stay. I always felt the talent was there. It's just how hard you work and how much you want to learn."

No Sophomore Slump for Pujols

As the 2002 season approached, Pujols signed a one-year contract that increased his salary from the major league minimum of $200,000 to $600,000. Not satisfied with his rookie success, he continued to work hard in spring training. "Last year I came in trying to make the club, and that's the same attitude I had this year," he explained. "There's always someone ready to take your spot. That's how it is and that's how I'll be thinking as long as God lets me play this game."

From the beginning of the 2002 season, Pujols made it clear that his rookie season was no fluke. He ended up batting .314 with 34 home runs and 127 RBIs, while walking 72 times and reducing his strikeout total to 69. He thus became the only player in major league history to bat over .300, drive in at least 100 runs, score at least 100 runs, and hit at least 30 home runs in each of his first two seasons. His impressive performance helped him to finish second to Barry Bonds in the voting for the National League MVP award.

Pujols demonstrated a remarkable combination of power, versatility, and consistency at the plate. He attributed his success as a hitter to his ability to recall pitchers' tendencies, recognize pitches, and make adjustments to his stance and swing as needed. "I've been blessed. I don't know how. The main thing is I can read a pitcher. I can make adjustments," he noted. "That's how you become a good hitter, when you can tell yourself what you're doing wrong and correct it the next at-bat. You don't want to do the same thing in three at-bats, then do something different the last at-bat. By then, it's too late. You want to make adjustments your first at-bat. You don't have to wait until somebody else corrects it. Sometimes it's better for people outside to say something, but 90 percent of the time I know what I'm doing wrong."

Pujols also continued to impress his Cardinals teammates and coaches with his preparation and desire to improve. He watched hours of videotape of different pitchers in order to study their movements. He also warmed up before each game by doing a long series of hitting drills, including some that were recommended to him by Texas Rangers star Alex Rodriguez. Although being a student of the game contributed to Pujols's success, his natural ability was undoubtedly an important factor as well.

Ichiro Suzuki (left) of the Seattle Mariners and Pujols (right) pose with trophies they received for being the top vote getters for the American and National leagues, respectively, for the 2003 All-Star Game.

"He's rare," said Cardinals' hitting coach Mitchell Page. "You look at that and you think of names like [Ted] Williams, [Rod] Carew, and [George] Brett, guys with beautiful, pure swings. Swings like his don't happen very often. It's a gift."

Pujols' terrific season helped steer the Cardinals to a 97-65 record and their third straight National League Central Division crown. St. Louis then swept the Diamondbacks in three straight games to advance to the National League Championship Series (NLCS). But Pujols and his teammates fell short in their bid for a World Series appearance, falling in five games to the San Francisco Giants.

2003 National League Batting Champion

As good as Pujols was in his first two major league seasons, he set a new standard for himself in 2003. Once again he led the National League in several offensive categories all year. Some fans hoped he would become the first player since Carl Yastrzemski in 1967 to achieve a Triple Crown (leading the league in batting average, RBIs, and home runs in the same season), but he fell 4 home runs and 17 RBIs short of this feat. Pujols did post the season's longest hitting streak, though, at 30 games. The streak, which was broken only when he spent five days sick with the flu, was the longest posted by a Cardinal player since 1950. In recognition of his success, Pujols became the top vote-getter in either league for the All-Star Game.

The Cardinals fell short in their bid for a fourth consecutive divisional championship. But St. Louis fans could take heart in another stellar performance by their team's superstar. By the end of the 2003 season, Pujols had posted a league-leading .359 batting average to claim the National League batting title. He also led the league in runs scored (137), hits (212), and total bases (394), and ranked second in slugging percentage and third in on-base percentage. Pujols added an impressive 43 home runs and 124 RBIs, which made him the only player in major league history to hit over .300 with at least 30 home runs, 100 RBIs, and 100 runs scored for three straight seasons. He also reduced his strikeout total to an amazing total of 65 in 591 at-bats, for an average of one strikeout in every 9 times he came up to the

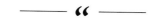

"I've worked my butt off. I want to get better in the outfield, and I'm pretty happy where I stand right now. This past season, I got to balls in the outfield that . . . before, I couldn't get to."

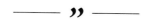

plate. In honor of his achievements, Pujols received *Sporting News* Player of the Year honors for 2003. "Plain and simple, no one has ever done what this guy has done," said Cardinals broadcaster Mike Shannon. "He's like Magellan. Nobody's ever been in these waters before."

The 2003 season marked the first time since joining the major leagues that Pujols was able to focus on playing one defensive position. After the Cardinals acquired third baseman Scott Rolen in July, Pujols spent the rest of the season in left field. He felt that the experience helped him to improve his fielding. "I've worked my butt off," he noted. "I want to get better in the outfield, and I'm pretty happy where I stand right now. This past season, I got to balls in the outfield that . . . before, I couldn't get to." During the off-season, however, the Cardinals traded first baseman Tino Martinez and announced that Pujols would move from outfield to first base. Since Pujols was a natural infielder, his coaches felt that this position would reduce his chance of injury and allow him to concentrate on his hitting.

As the Cardinals entered spring training for 2004, team management began working to sign Pujols to a long-term contract. In February 2004 Pujols signed a seven-year, $100 million contract—making him the highest-paid player in Cardinals' history. "His accomplishments in his first three seasons are unmatched in the history of the game," said team co-owner Bill DeWitt. "Having reached this agreement, the Cardinals and their fans can now rest assured that Albert Pujols will serve as a cornerstone for the Cardinals for many years to come."

Pujols started out slowly in the 2004 season. He went through the first hitting slump of his career, which caused his batting average to dip below .300 at the end of May. But then his wife—an avid softball player—watched some videotapes of his swing and suggested that he narrow his batting stance. The next day, Cardinals' batting coach Mitchell Page noticed the same thing. Pujols made the adjustment and immediately went on an offensive tear, hitting six home runs in the next nine games. By August he had increased his average to .318, whacked 33 home runs, and regained his former RBI-swatting form. In late August Pujols became only the fourth player in major league history to knock in 100 runs in each of their first four seasons.

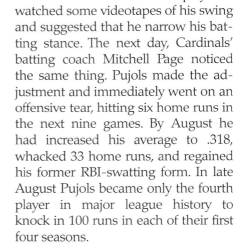

"One of the mistakes a lot of young players make is that once they get to the big leagues, they think, 'That's it,' and they don't work that hard," observed Pujols. "But you have to work extra hard to get better. The older you get, the more you have to work to get better."

Working Hard to Be the Best

By 2004 Pujols was widely considered to be among the best hitters in the game. In fact, Cardinals' Coach Tony La Russa—who has coached many great players in his 30 years in the majors—called Pujols the best he had ever seen. "I watch Pujols day in and day out the three years he's been here. The stuff this guy does, the quality at-bats, the pitches he does things with. I mean, it's up there with the great players," La Russa said. "Now will he keep doing it for the next 12 to 15 years? That'll be the test. He's got great hands. He trusts his hands. He's courageous. He's relentless in his work. I've said for our fans to appreciate what they have. When he plays the game to win, he's really playing the game to win. He's not playing to generate stats, which is very special in today's baseball. He's got it figured, man. Stats just happen."

In 2004 Pujols became the fourth player in major league history to knock in 100 runs in each of his first four seasons.

Former Cardinals player and current team broadcaster Mike Shannon also paid tribute to Pujols: "It's no accident what we're seeing. This is the whole package. Talent-wise, we all know [he has] that. But he has the desire. He has the professionalism. He has the hunger. He has the humility. And to top all that, he's the smartest player I've ever seen come along. OK, [Willie] Mays was the smartest player I've ever seen. But I've never seen a smarter guy with less experience. . . . If he stays healthy and keeps performing like he's performing, which you expect, he's going to keep breaking records and do things that nobody's done before."

Despite the praise and awards he has received, Pujols remains humble and continues to dedicate himself to improving his game. "I know I'm a good hitter, but I don't think I'm the greatest hitter in the game right now.

There are a lot of guys who are great hitters. It's nice what the media says, but you can't think about that stuff. You have to stay humble and go play the game," he explained. "One of the mistakes a lot of young players make is that once they get to the big leagues, they think, 'That's it,' and they don't work that hard. But you have to work extra hard to get better. The older you get, the more you have to work to get better. I'm still working hard every day."

MARRIAGE AND FAMILY

Pujols met his wife, Deidre (known as Dee Dee), at a Latin dance club in Kansas City. He was 18 and still in high school at the time, while she was 21 and a college graduate. She had also recently given birth to a daughter, Isabella, with Down syndrome (a genetic disorder that generally occurs in one of every 800 births and results in various physical problems and moderate mental retardation). Despite the difference in their ages and situations, the couple began dating and soon fell in love. From the beginning of their relationship, Pujols has treated Isabella as his own daughter. He fed and changed her as an infant, cared for her when Dee Dee had to work, and accompanied her to doctor appointments. "I feel like I'm her dad," he stated. "Sometimes I don't even think of her having the Down syndrome anymore. She's so cute. I just look at her like a normal baby."

Pujols married Dee Dee on New Year's Day in 2000, and he adopted Isabella a short time later. Since he was a poorly paid minor league ballplayer at the time, money was tight for the young family. They had a son, Alberto Jose (known as A.J.), in January 2001, shortly before Pujols's stellar rookie year with the Cardinals. "He's really excited to have this little baseball player," Dee Dee said of A.J.'s birth. "Albert didn't know what to think, he was so much in awe. That was probably one of the best moments in his life. If he accomplishes anything, moments like that will still be considered the best."

The Pujols family lives in suburban St. Louis. They spend the offseason in Florida and eventually hope to buy a second home in Miami. Pujols takes every available opportunity to emphasize the importance of family in his life. "God first, my family second, my career third," he stated. "I try to spend as much time as possible with God and my family. That's more important than anything I am doing in baseball."

HOBBIES AND OTHER INTERESTS

Pujols claims that he does not have time for hobbies. "I spend time with my family," he noted. "That's my hobby. That's it. Family and baseball." He is

*Pujols and his son A.J. walking to the batting cage at the Cardinals'
spring training complex in Florida.*

active in charity work, though, and sponsors an annual celebrity golf tournament to benefit the Down Syndrome Association of Greater St. Louis.

AWARDS AND HONORS

National League Rookie of the Year (Baseball Writers' Association of
America): 2001
National League All-Star Team: 2001-2004
Major League Player of the Year (Players' League): 2003
Major League Player of the Year (*Sporting News*): 2003
National League Batting Champion: 2003
Hank Aaron Award as Best Offensive Player in the National League: 2003

FURTHER READING

Periodicals

Baseball Digest, Dec. 2001, p.46; Nov. 2002, p.48; Oct. 2003, p.22; Feb. 2004,
p.38
Current Biography Yearbook, 2004
Kansas City (Mo.) Star, Oct. 9, 2001, p.C1; June 27, 2004, p.C1
St. Louis Post-Dispatch, May 20, 2001, p.D1; Mar. 30, 2003, p.4; Feb. 21,
2004, p.3
Sporting News, June 23, 2003, p.16; Oct. 27, 2003, p.8
Sports Illustrated, Apr. 16, 2001, p.48; Oct. 1, 2001, p.44; June 30, 2003, p.32
Sports Illustrated for Kids, June 1, 2003, p.36
USA Today, May 22, 2001, p.C1
Washington Post, Aug. 24, 2003, p.E1

Online Databases

Biography Resource Center Online, 2002

ADDRESS

Albert Pujols
St. Louis Cardinals
250 Stadium Plaza
St. Louis, MO 63102

WORLD WIDE WEB SITE

http://stlouis.cardinals.mlb.com

Michael Strahan 1971-

American Professional Football Player with the
New York Giants
Five-Time Pro Bowl Defensive End and 2001 NFL
Defensive Player of the Year
Holder of the NFL Single-Season Record for
Quarterback Sacks

BIRTH

Michael Anthony Strahan (*STRAY-han*) was born on November 21, 1971, in Houston, Texas. His father, Gene Strahan, was an officer in the U.S. Army. "My dad was a paratrooper, the

115

82nd Airborne Division," Michael explained. "When something goes wrong, they were among the first to go when the country needed defending. Any time you see somebody putting their lives on the line for people they don't even know, that's incredible." After Gene retired from the military in 1985, he and his wife, Louise, started their own transport business. Michael is the youngest of six children in his family. He has three brothers and two sisters.

YOUTH

The Strahan family moved around a lot during Michael's early youth, as his father was transferred between various military bases. Michael played in his first youth football league at age seven, when his father was stationed in Fort Bragg, North Carolina, but his interest in the sport did not take root until several years later.

In 1980, when Michael was nine years old, his family moved to Mannheim, Germany—an area near Frankfurt that was the site of a U.S. military base. Although Michael lived in what was then West Germany for the next nine years, he never learned to speak the language. "I can order food, but that's about it," he admitted. "But almost everybody in Germany can speak English, so instead of letting me struggle, they'd just talk to me in English." Still, he enjoyed his years in Germany. "It's a great culture, the German culture," he explained. "Everything is so clean. It's so relaxing. In the States, everything is go-go-go."

Michael did not show much interest in athletics until he reached his teen years. "When I was 13 years old, I was a little chubby," he recalled. "My brothers called me BOB, which was short for 'Booty on Back.' They made fun of me and it made me start working out. I was up at 5:30 doing my Jane Fonda tapes. I just wanted to improve myself. I wasn't even playing football yet."

Determined to get in shape, Michael began working out with his father, who did intensive physical training for the 82nd Airborne and also participated in Armed Services boxing tournaments. Michael and his father ran five miles every morning, lifted weights at the base gym, completed military obstacle courses, and practiced boxing. "I never pushed him to come along on those morning runs," his father noted. "We'd be up in the woods trying to stay in shape for this elite outfit, and the next day, he would be right back there. I never asked him to come to the gym. He would ride his bike over to my office. I can't explain it but I know how he felt. Something was gnawing at him to make himself better."

Over the years, Michael developed an extraordinary combination of strength and speed. At the same time, football gradually floated back into his life. Although few opportunities existed to play American football in Germany, he enjoyed watching "Monday Night Football" games with his father. They would go to bed early each Monday night during the NFL season so that they could wake up to see the game at 3:00 a.m. German time. Michael did not know much about the game, except that he liked it.

EDUCATION

Michael attended several different elementary schools in the United States before he moved to Germany at the age of nine. He completed most of the rest of his schooling in Mannheim. In the fall of 1988, however, his parents decided to send him back to the United States. They believed that he had the athletic talent to earn a college scholarship playing football. "My dad saw something in me, but I'm not sure what it was," Michael related. "When I was in high school in Germany, he told me I was going to make it to pro football. I couldn't believe it because I wasn't even playing football at the time. He told me I was going to get a scholarship. It was a dream of his, and through his will, I've been able to accomplish it."

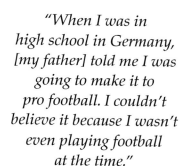

"When I was in high school in Germany, [my father] told me I was going to make it to pro football. I couldn't believe it because I wasn't even playing football at the time."

Michael returned to Houston, Texas, to live with his uncle Art Strahan, a former NFL defensive lineman. From the time he arrived in the United States, he had a hard time adjusting to American culture. "I was so naive it was incredible," he admitted. "I knew absolutely nothing. We drove past this building that said 'Drugs' on it, and I couldn't believe it. I thought, the drug dealers have signs! How can they not bust 'em? I didn't know about drug stores."

For the first half of his senior year of high school, Michael played football at Westbury High School in Houston. His uncle gave him some pointers before the season began. "My uncle taught me how to work and how to be tough," he remembered. "When I was in Houston, he'd take me in the front yard and show me pass-rush drills, how to use my hands. He'd hit me a little too hard, but I wouldn't tell him. He played a big role in my development."

117

Michael only played in eight games for Westbury High, but his combination of size, strength, and speed impressed recruiters at several colleges. True to his father's predictions, he earned a full athletic scholarship to attend Texas Southern University (TSU). As soon as he accepted the scholarship offer, though, he left Texas and returned to his family in Germany. He finished his senior year at the small, private Mannheim American High School, graduating in 1989. "I graduated in a class of two, and I was not the valedictorian," he noted. "But I can always say I finished in the top two in my class."

Strahan then returned to the United States. He attended Texas Southern and played Division 1-AA football for the next four years (Division 1-AA is a class below Division 1-A football, the class in which major public and private universities compete). A business management major, he left school in 1992 — before earning his degree — to play in the NFL. He later took classes toward completing his degree at Fairleigh Dickinson University in New Jersey.

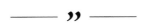

"I hadn't grown up in the States and I didn't understand or like the lifestyle. I didn't know anything about American football really, didn't know how to play my position."

CAREER HIGHLIGHTS

College — Texas Southern University

Strahan was miserable during his first semester of college. He struggled to fit into American culture and meet his responsibilities as a student and athlete. He also missed his family back in Germany. Following his freshman season at Texas Southern, he informed his parents that he had no interest in returning to the United States. "I always paid attention to my dad, but in my first year of college, I thought he'd been dreaming. I was away from home, and my parents were in Germany. On Thanksgiving and Christmas, I'd see the others go home, and I'd be sitting in the dorm room by myself. It wasn't a good feeling," he recalled. "After that first semester of college, I had taken everything out of my dorm room because I was never going back. I hadn't grown up in the States and I didn't understand or like the lifestyle. I didn't know anything about American football really, didn't know how to play my position."

After a long talk with his father, however, Strahan realized that he was throwing away a valuable opportunity. He decided to return to Texas

Strahan rushes into the backfield of the Los Angeles Rams during 1994 action.

Southern and give football his best effort. "A lightbulb clicked on," he remembered. "I thought, 'Your mom and dad aren't going to take care of you forever. If you're going to go back to play football, try to be the best at it. Don't be satisfied with being just another player.'" Gene Strahan never doubted that his son would make the right decision. "We had spent a lot of time together and he was homesick," he explained. "He had to find his own way, that's all. Mike was not going to quit. I knew that. And he knew that."

Upon returning to college, Strahan dedicated himself to becoming the best football player he could be. He spent a great deal of time learning about the game and preparing himself both mentally and physically. Before long, he emerged as one of the biggest stars ever to come out of Texas Southern. "Every year, I just kept improving a little more," he said. As a junior defensive end in 1991, Strahan led the Southwestern Athletic Conference (SWAC) with 14.5 sacks. (A sack occurs when a defensive player tackles the opposing quarterback behind the line of scrimmage, resulting in a loss of yardage for the offense. Players receive credit for a half-sack when they are partially responsible for stopping the quarterback.) Strahan's performance earned him a spot on the All-Conference team and led to his selection as the Black College Defensive Player of the Year.

As a senior in 1992, Strahan posted 19 sacks and 62 tackles. His 41.5 career sacks established a new school record. He was named Black College Defensive Player of the Year, SWAC Defensive Player of the Year, and an NCAA All-American. Even though he played for a small college, many people believed that he had the potential to become a star in the NFL. "Michael's self-motivated. He's got a great work ethic. You could tell he was something special," said J.W. Harper, his defensive line coach at TSU. "His motor was always running. He had a quick first step. He could run, and he could keep people off his feet. We put him through every drill imaginable, and he excelled at all of them. By his junior year, opponents were having to build their game plan around him. That's when I knew he had a chance to play in the NFL."

NFL — The New York Giants

The New York Giants selected Strahan in the second round of the 1993 NFL draft, with the 40th overall pick. He was thrilled to have an opportunity to play professional football, but he was initially nervous about living in New York City. "When I went to New York after the draft, I wouldn't leave the hotel for three days. I was scared," he admitted. "All I'd heard about was if you go outside in New York, don't look up. They'll think you're a tourist and mug you. I just looked out the hotel window. It took me a while to adjust."

As his rookie season got underway, Strahan was determined to contribute to the Giants' success. "I expect a lot out of myself," he stated. "I expect to help the team the first year in some way. From everything I see here, I'm not an every-down player, but when I learn the position and get stronger, I will play every down. I'm a quick learner and I have good work habits."

Strahan recorded his first and only sack of the season during his first NFL game, but he suffered foot and ankle injuries that limited his action to nine games. The Giants posted an 11-5 record that year to finish second in the NFC East Division. They beat the Minnesota Vikings in a Wild Card playoff game but lost to the San Francisco 49ers in the divisional playoff.

During his second season in 1994, Strahan started 15 of 16 games as the Giants' right defensive end. He made his first professional start on September 4 against Philadelphia, and he sacked Eagles quarterback Randall Cunningham in that game. Strahan finished the year with 38 tackles (25 solo) and 4.5 sacks, but the Giants only managed a 9-7 record and missed the playoffs.

In 1995 Strahan once again started 15 games. He ended up with 58 tackles (48 solo) and 7.5 sacks during his third pro season, and he also forced 3

Strahan celebrates after registering a sack in a 1995 tilt against the Washington Redskins.

fumbles. Highlights of the year included his first career interception during a game against the Kansas City Chiefs, his first 3-sack game against the Green Bay Packers, and his first blocked punt against Philadelphia. Unfortunately, the Giants limped to a 5-11 record and missed the playoffs again.

Prior to the start of the 1996 season, Giants coaches decided to move Strahan to left defensive end. Although he recognized that the change was necessary due to injuries on the defensive line, Strahan remained a bit apprehensive about it. "I've been driving my car on the right side for three

Strahan's strength and agility made him a difficult challenge for opposing offensive linemen to defend.

or four years, and now they slapped the steering wheel on the left and told me to drive on the other side of the street. I have to see how it is before I can judge it," he noted. "There are so many different things I have to do and learn, it's going to take some time." Strahan started all 16 games on the left side that year, posting 62 tackles (52 solo) and 5 sacks and forcing 1 fumble. The Giants played poorly once again, however. The team posted a 6-10 record and missed the playoffs for the third straight year. "It seemed like every game it was a new ending to a bad movie," Strahan stated at season's end. "There's nothing worse than when you're watching the playoffs on TV. This team is better than that."

Becoming a Pro Bowl Defensive End

During his fifth pro season in 1997, Strahan raised his game to an all-new level. He tied for third in the NFL with 14 sacks, made 68 tackles (46 solo), forced a fumble, and recovered a fumble. His performance earned him his first career trip to the NFL Pro Bowl. "I didn't grow up playing this game, and I'm still learning," he said at the time. "Out here, I feel like a kid because these guys have been playing since they were young. I'm trying to emulate them. It's unbelievable how it's worked out for me. To go from not playing to having a chance to play college football to ending up in the Pro Bowl, I couldn't ask for more." The Giants improved to 10-5-1 that season and won the NFC East Division, but lost in the first round of the playoffs to the Minnesota Vikings.

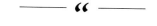

"I promised my mom I was going to keep the ball for her if I scored a touchdown, so now I've got to put it in a box and send it to Germany."

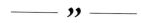

When the 1998 season kicked off, Strahan recognized that opposing coaches had taken note of his growth as a player. He often faced double-teams, and many opponents chose to avoid him altogether by running plays toward the other side of the field. Nonetheless, Strahan still led his team in sacks with 15. In addition, he recorded 67 tackles (53 solo), forced 2 fumbles, and returned an interception 24 yards for his first career touchdown against the Washington Redskins. "I promised my mom I was going to keep the ball for her if I scored a touchdown, so now I've got to put it in a box and send it to Germany," he said afterward. "I think this game was on TV back there. They were probably jumping around the house. Neighbors may have called the police."

Under the leadership of Strahan and his teammate Jessie Armstead — both of whom were named to the 1998 Pro Bowl — New York's defense emerged as one of the most powerful in the league. But the Giants only managed an 8-8 record and failed to make the playoffs. Midway through the season, Strahan and Armstead made the controversial decision to walk uninvited into a meeting of the team's offensive players. Strahan and Armstead then called on their teammates to play harder and execute better. "We were very upset with what they did," recalled running back Tiki Barber, one of the leaders of the Giants offense. "We thought it was out of line. But I have to admit, it worked."

Shortly before the start of the 1999 season, Strahan signed a four-year contract worth $32 million. His average salary of $8 million per year made him the richest defensive lineman in NFL history. Unfortunately, his seventh pro season turned out to be the most difficult of his career. Beginning in the preseason, Strahan suffered a series of injuries—including two hyperextended elbows, a pulled quadriceps muscle, a separated shoulder, back spasms, and a torn thumb ligament that eventually required surgery—that limited his effectiveness on the field. When he failed to record a sack in the first four games of the season, fans and reporters began to question whether his big contract had made him lazy.

Frustrated by his own lack of production and the team's mediocre performance, Strahan lashed out publicly. Late in the season, following a three-game losing streak, he gave an interview in which he criticized the Giants offense and the head coach, Jim Fassel. Since Fassel was out of town attending his mother's funeral at the time, Strahan was condemned by many observers as an insensitive jerk. Fassel returned and made Strahan apologize to his teammates. The whole controversial incident convinced Strahan to stop talking to the media for the rest of the season, but it did not seem to affect his play. He finished the season with 60 tackles (41 solo), 5.5 sacks, 2 fumble recoveries, and an interception that he returned 44 yards for a touchdown. He was voted to the Pro Bowl for the third time, but the Giants finished 7-9 and missed the playoffs.

Leading His Team to the Super Bowl

As the 2000 season got underway, Strahan was healthy for the first time in a year. He acknowledged that the 1999 campaign had been a trying one for him. "Last year, I didn't have much fun," he admitted. "If I could have retired last year, I would have. I was mad at the world. I hated football."

Strahan finally improved his attitude and his performance with the help of two people close to him. His wife Jean suggested that he change his approach to the game and try to have more fun. Then his teammate Jessie Armstead pointed out that he was focusing so much of his energy on trying to sack the quarterback that he was leaving the rest of the defensive unit vulnerable. "I admit it, sacks were just messing with my head," he stated. "I was obsessed with them, I was. I don't know when I realized that, but I just knew it had to change. I'd expect to get a sack, then I wouldn't and I'd be miserable. This year, sacks come and go, and I'm doing my best. But

Strahan recovers a fumble to score a rare defensive touchdown in this December 2001 game against the Seattle Seahawks.

when I look over and see that I have two guys on me, three guys on me, there's nothing I can do about it. I'm not going to sweat it anymore."

Turning his emphasis away from the sack helped Strahan become a more complete defensive player. Although he finished the 2000 season with only 9.5 sacks, he added 66 tackles (50 solo) and 4 fumble recoveries and anchored one of the top run-defenses in the NFL. Thanks in part to Strahan's leadership, the Giants improved their record to 12-4 and finished first in the NFC East Division. "The change in Michael had been un-believable," said Fassel. "There is no doubt in my mind that he has had a Pro Bowl year. But it's not just that. He works as hard as anyone on the team. He had played hard every snap this year—training camp, games, practices, you name it. He has been one of the guys who has set the tone for our season."

For his part, Strahan expressed satisfaction with the way the season un-folded. "I think this is probably the best that I've played overall in my ca-reer," he said afterward. "I've had years when I've had more sacks. For a lot of people that's more important. For me, winning is more important. I'll tell you what, I'm happy."

In the NFC divisional playoff, the Giants defeated Philadelphia 20-10. They went on to crush Minnesota 41-0 in the divisional finals and advance to the Super Bowl. Unfortunately, New York met a superior team in the Baltimore Ravens. Despite Strahan's 6 tackles and 1.5 sacks, the Giants lost the NFL championship by a score of 34-7.

Setting the NFL Single-Season Sack Record

During the 2001 season, Strahan continued to pursue his strategy of being a complete defensive player. "I go into games not thinking about sacks, but thinking about being disruptive in any way I can," he explained. He started out slowly, without recording a sack in the Giants' first two games. But he rallied to post 13.5 sacks in the next five games, including four in one game against the St. Louis Rams. It soon became clear that he had a chance to break the NFL's all-time single-season record of 22 sacks, which had been set by Mark Gastineau of the New York Jets in 1984.

Strahan had an outstanding year in many other respects as well. He made 73 tackles (60 solo) and forced a career-high 7 fumbles. He also scored the third touchdown of his career on a 13-yard fumble recovery against the Seattle Seahawks. But his individual effort was partially overshadowed by the fact that—after appearing in the Super Bowl the previous season—the Giants stumbled to a disappointing 7-9 record and failed to make the playoffs.

Strahan's attempt to break the sack record came down to the last game of the season against Green Bay. The Packers' offense contained Strahan for most of the game, and many fans expected his sack total to remain at 21.5, just a half-sack short of the record. But with 2:45 left in the fourth quarter, and Green Bay ahead 34-25, Packers quarterback Brett Favre rolled to his right, slipped, and fell down behind the line of scrimmage with Strahan in pursuit. Strahan fell on top of Favre and received credit for the sack.

Strahan registered an NFL-record 22 sacks in the 2001 campaign.

Some people expressed disappointment at the manner in which Strahan collected the sack that broke Gastineau's all-time record. Critics claimed that Favre took a dive and gave the record to Strahan, although the quarterback later denied it and blamed a broken play. NFL commentator John Madden expressed disgust at the Giants' reaction to Strahan's record, which he said indicated too much emphasis on individual statistics. "The Giants go to play a football game against the Green Bay Packers. They lose the game. The next thing I see is a guy hugging his coach. I see another guy coming down on the field and kissing him. And they lost," Madden stated. "They were in the Super Bowl a year ago and they had a crappy season. And guys are kissing and hugging each other and stuff. And for what?"

*Strahan tapes up his fingers
prior to practice.*

Strahan tried not to concern himself with the controversy surrounding the sack record. "If somebody doesn't like it, everybody has the opportunity to break it," he noted. "One thing I've learned is that the more success you have, the more people hate to see it." He was gratified when the former record holder expressed his support. "No sack is a gimme," said Gastineau. "The record [Strahan] set today, he deserves."

Contracts and Controversy

Controversy continued to surround Strahan during the offseason. For several months he refused to sign a contract extension with the Giants because he wanted more of his salary to be guaranteed (still payable if he were to be injured or released by the team). Team management was reluctant to meet Strahan's demand because guaranteed salaries count against the salary cap (the maximum total that each NFL team can pay its players), which could limit the Giants' ability to sign promising rookies or free agents. Strahan's position led some members of the media, as well as his teammate Tiki Barber, to accuse the star defensive end of being selfish and hurting the team. Shortly before the 2002 season began, however, Giants management met Strahan's demands and gave him a seven-year contract extension worth $46 million.

Strahan started all 16 games for the Giants in 2002, marking the fourth straight year he started every contest and the seventh year in a row that he did not miss a game. He posted 70 tackles (55 solo) and 11 sacks, added 3 forced fumbles and 1 fumble recovery. His strong performance led to his fifth career selection to the Pro Bowl. Although the Giants made it to the NFC Wild Card playoffs, they lost to San Francisco.

Strahan had another strong year in 2003, recording 76 tackles (61 solo) and 18.5 sacks. He thus brought his career sack total to 113.5 and earned his sixth trip to the Pro Bowl. Despite his efforts, however, the Giants struggled. They lost the last 8 games of the season on their way to a dismal

4-12 record. Coach Jim Fassel was fired at the end of the season and re-placed by Tom Coughlin.

The new head coach made several roster changes during the offseason. Strahan expressed surprise at Coughlin's decision to release quarterback Kerry Collins and hand rookie Eli Manning the reins of the Giants' of-fense. Though he admitted that Manning was talented, Strahan worried that the young quarterback would not be ready to run an NFL offense in his first pro season. As it turned out, Coughlin benched Manning in favor of veteran Kurt Warner at the start of the 2004 season.

Sacking the Opposition

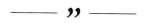

As he entered his 12th season of pro-fessional football, Strahan dismissed any notions that he might be slowing down. "I am in that weight room every day, on the treadmill every day, sit-ups every day, got to keep it tight," he stated. "I enjoy it. If you put it in your head that you love what you do and you are going to enjoy and do it, it's not hard."

> "[Sacking the quarterback is] the best feeling in the world," said Strahan. "The only thing you hear is complete silence during the play, then after the sack, it's like somebody has the radio up on max volume. Instant adrenaline rush. And then you jump up like you just won the Lotto."

At 6 feet, 5 inches and 275 pounds, Strahan is fast enough to catch speedy quarterbacks behind the line of scrim-mage. But he is also smart and strong enough to push around offensive line-men who outweigh him by 50 to 100 pounds. "When you come off the ball, you're sizing the offensive lineman up, judging him," he explained. "It's like chess. You have to set a guy up. I'm looking to see if what I set him up with earlier is working. I'm just thinking, I gotta get him pushed back toward that quarterback and then get off him at the right time. If I beat him badly and I've got a lock on the quarterback, I'm thinking, Explode and drive to the quarterback. Don't slow up, because if you slow up, you'll get there right when he throws it, or the tackle will cut you from behind, or some-thing like that."

Strahan describes sacking an opposing quarterback as "the perfect mo-ment in life." "When you hit, you feel him go uuffff," he added. "It's the best feeling in the world. Oh man, it feels great. The only thing you hear is complete silence during the play, then after the sack, it's like somebody

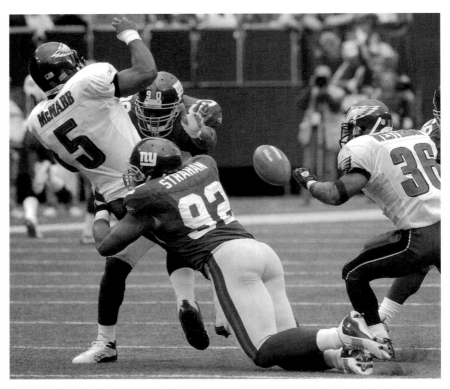

Philadephia Eagles quarterback Donovan McNabb (5) fumbles after being run down by Strahan (92) in this October 2003 contest.

has the radio up on max volume. Instant adrenaline rush. And then you jump up like you just won the Lotto."

MARRIAGE AND FAMILY

Strahan married his first wife, Wanda—an American he met in Germany—during his college years at Texas Southern. The marriage produced a daughter, Tanita, and a son, Michael Jr., before ending in divorce. Strahan met his second wife, Jean Muggli, at a charity event in 1994. They were married in July 1999, and in the summer of 2004 they told a reporter that they were expecting twins.

Michael and Jean Strahan live in a 22,000-square-foot, Greek Revival-style mansion on three acres of land in Montclair, New Jersey. It has 12 bedrooms, 7 bathrooms, and 113 windows, many of which provide a view of the New York skyline 15 miles away. "In this house, you're staring out at

Manhattan all the time," Strahan explained. "Some days I do come home and just stand there and look at the city — New York City. It's one of those things you never get tired of. You walk through the house with the lights out and look out and go, 'Wow!'"

Strahan's house was built in 1906. Since he and his wife bought it in 2000, it has been undergoing a complete restoration. "I love old things. I like things with character," Strahan noted. "In this day, so much is generic, and I don't want to have a generic life. I don't want to be a generic person, and I don't want to live around generic things." The Strahans share their home with three dogs, Tasha, Katie, and Stella.

HOBBIES AND OTHER INTERESTS

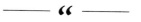

In his spare time, Strahan enjoys collecting antiques to restore and furnish his home. "It's a good way to get out, spend some time with your wife. And it's interesting. You find something, you research it, make sure it's what you want, and then you're part of the history of that piece," he explained. "The best part is the thrill of the hunt. I like to look for the piece, figure out where it's going to go. I try to visualize how I want the room to look and find something that suits it." In 2003 Strahan opened his house for public tours to help raise funds for the Montclair Junior League.

"It's a great feeling to walk into a room and see kids' eyes light up," Strahan said. "They respond to what you say. They'll listen to you more than their parents. I enjoy it because kids are so honest. We have a responsibility to them. I want to give them hope. I want to bring awareness to the cause."

Strahan supports a wide variety of charitable causes, including the American Cancer Society, Children's Miracle Network, and People for the Ethical Treatment of Animals. One of his favorite organizations is Housing Enterprises for the Less Privileged (HELP). "They offer temporary housing, jobs, counseling," he noted. "It's to get people back on their feet, and give them skills so they don't fall back into homelessness. It helps people who want to help themselves."

Strahan helps serve Thanksgiving dinner at a homeless shelter every fall, and he takes homeless children to his football camps every summer. "It's a great feeling to walk into a room and see kids' eyes light up," he acknowledged. "They respond to what you say. They'll listen to you more than their parents. I enjoy it because kids are so honest. We have a responsibility to them. I want to give them hope. I want to bring awareness to the cause."

Strahan also owns Michael Strahan Enterprises, a sports and entertainment business based in Mannheim, Germany. One of the company's goals is to implement football programs in German school systems. "That is my backup plan," he stated. "Football is only one part of my life. When it's over I'll definitely be doing something else."

HONORS AND AWARDS

Southwestern Athletic Conference Player of the Year: 1991, 1992
Black College Defensive Player of the Year: 1991, 1992
NCAA All-American (Associated Press): 1992
NFL Pro Bowl: 1997, 1998, 1999, 2001, 2002, 2003
NFL Player of the Year (*Sports Illustrated*): 2001
NFL Defensive Player of the Year (Associated Press): 2001
NFL Defensive Player of the Year (*Pro Football Weekly*): 2001
NFL Single-Season Sack Record: 2001

FURTHER READING

Books

Contemporary Black Biography, Vol. 35, 2002
I Love You, Mom! A Celebration of Our Mothers and Their Gifts to Us, 2002
Who's Who among African Americans, 2004

Periodicals

GQ, Dec. 2002, p.66
Houston Chronicle, Jan. 31, 1998, Sports, p.1
New Jersey Monthly, Mar. 2004, p.33
New York Daily News, Aug. 31, 1997, Special, p.9
New York Times, May 2, 1993, p.S2; Aug. 2, 1994, p.B12; Dec. 25, 2002, p.D2
Newark (N.J.) Star-Ledger, July 20, 1996, p.37; Dec. 17, 2001, p.1
Sporting News, Nov. 12, 2001, p.48; Dec. 10, 2001, p.20
Sports Illustrated, Jan. 29, 2001, p.46; Dec. 17, 2001, p.74
Sports Illustrated for Kids, Mar. 1, 2002, p.8; Nov. 1, 2002, p.35

Online Articles

http://www.rlrassociates.net/clients
(RLR Associates Ltd., "A Fitting Scene," Oct. 21, 2001; "Out of the Woods, into the Spotlight," Nov. 19, 2001)

http://www.nfl.com/insider
  (*NFL Insider,* "Strahan Home Improvement a Labor of Love,"Oct. 3, 2002)
http://www.newsday.com/sports/football/giants
  (*Newsday,* "This Giant House,"May 4, 2003)
http://www.usatoday.com/sports/football/nfl/giants
  (*USA Today,* "No Place Like Home for the Strahans,"May 5, 2003)
http://casadesign4living.com/current/giant.html
  (*Casa Design for Living,* "Into the House of a Giant,"2003)

Online Databases

Biography Resource Center, 2004, articles from *Contemporary Black Biography,* 2002, and *Who's Who among African Americans,* 2004

ADDRESS

Michael Strahan
New York Giants
Giants Stadium
East Rutherford, NJ 07073

WORLD WIDE WEB SITES

http://www.giants.com
http://www.nfl.com
http://www.nflplayers.com

Teresa Weatherspoon 1965-

American Professional Basketball Player with the
Los Angeles Sparks
Two-Time WNBA Defensive Player of the Year and
Five-Time WNBA All-Star

BIRTH

Teresa Gaye Weatherspoon, known to her friends and fans alike
as "Spoon" or "T-Spoon," was born on December 8, 1965, in
Jasper, Texas. Her father, Charles Weatherspoon, played minor-
league baseball in the Minnesota Twins organization. Her mother, Rowena Weatherspoon, was a homemaker. Teresa is the

youngest of six children in her family. She has two older brothers, Charles Jr. ("June") and Michael, and three older sisters, Diana ("Dinky"), Carolyn ("K.K."), and Denise ("NeeCee").

YOUTH

Teresa has described her hometown of Pineland, Texas, as "so small that you don't have to use the telephone. All you have to do is yell out the door." She grew up playing basketball with her older brothers on a rough dirt court known as "the sandlot" across the street from their house. She later claimed that the rustic nature of the court helped her develop strong ballhandling skills. "I knew if I could dribble on all those bumps, I could dribble anywhere," she stated.

From the time she was a little girl, Teresa played basketball whenever she had the opportunity. She played in the mornings before school, in the afternoons, and every weekend. "I was always playing ball. Always. From grammar school until senior year of high school, any time I saw someone playing ball, I was there," she recalled. "I wanted to play at night, too, but there weren't any lights in the sandlot, so the game would end when you couldn't see anymore."

"I was always playing ball. Always. From grammar school until senior year of high school, any time I saw someone playing ball, I was there."

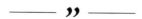

Teresa was usually the only girl playing in the sandlot. Her mother always allowed her to play with the boys, but her father initially resisted the idea. "My dad was really worried about me getting hurt, playing with guys who were a little more physical," she remembered. "But my dad came in early one day, and he saw me playing football—tackle football—with the guys. I tackled one guy, and I mean I *flushed* him to the ground, and then I looked in the doorway and I saw my dad, and I was like, 'Oh boy, I'm in trouble.' So I went in the house, and I said, 'Dad, I'm sorry I was out playing with the guys,' and he said, 'Hey, you really hit that guy.' When he saw just how physical I was, he was like, 'My baby can *play* with those guys.' After that he gave me no trouble at all."

Although the Weatherspoon family was poor, they worked together to get through the hard times. "There wasn't very much money when I was growing up, and there were six kids," Teresa related. "My parents separated, and my mother struggled to help us survive. Everyone in the family gave up some things he or she wanted to do in life. We sacrificed for each other to make it." She credits her mother for giving her the confidence and strength to pursue her dreams. "My mom always taught me to dream big and believe in myself. To believe—always believe," she noted. "When things get tough and obstacles are in the way, always believe. Always find a positive when negative things are coming."

EDUCATION

Weatherspoon attended West Sabine High School in Texas, where she was a star athlete as well as a top student. On the basketball court, she averaged 21.2 points per game and led her team to four district championships. Her dynamic play at point guard attracted large crowds to her high school games. Weatherspoon also excelled in the classroom, where her favorite subjects were math and English. When she graduated from West Sabine High in 1984, she was valedictorian of her class. Weatherspoon went on to attend Louisiana Technological University on a basketball scholarship. She graduated from college in 1988 with a degree in health and physical education.

———— " ————

"My mom always taught me to dream big and believe in myself. To believe—always believe," Weatherspoon recalled.

———— " ————

CAREER HIGHLIGHTS

College—The Louisiana Tech Lady Techsters

When Weatherspoon accepted the basketball scholarship to Louisiana Tech, she was thrilled to have an opportunity to play for Coach Leon Barmore, who had recently led the Lady Techsters to two NCAA national championships. The coach made his expectations clear right away, and he ended up changing the focus of her game. "When I got to college, the first thing Coach Barmore said was, 'If you want to play on this team, you got to guard somebody,'" she recalled. "Up till then, I had been more of an offensive player, but I wanted to play for him, because I thought he was the best, and I said, 'Hey, I can give you defense all day long.' And that's where I stood out, on the defensive end. It all goes back to him."

During her college career, Weatherspoon emerged as one of the best players in the country. She helped the Lady Techsters reach the NCAA championship game in both her junior and senior seasons. After losing in the finals in 1987, Weatherspoon was determined to claim the title in 1988. In the championship game, Louisiana Tech faced Auburn, which was led by star point guard Ruthie Bolton. Weatherspoon received the tough assignment of guarding Bolton, who scorched the Lady Techsters for 16 points in the first half. But Weatherspoon came back in the second half and used smothering defense to hold Bolton scoreless and force her to make six turnovers. Her performance helped the Lady Techsters win the game, 56-54, and claim the 1988 NCAA national championship.

Weatherspoon left Louisiana Tech as the school's career leader in steals (with 411) and assists (with 958). She also scored 1,087 career points and grabbed 533 rebounds. She received a number of prestigious awards at the conclusion of her senior season, including the

Weatherspoon (11) used stifling defense to help lift the Lady Techsters to the 1988 NCAA women's basketball crown.

Broderick Cup as the nation's top female collegiate athlete and the Wade Trophy as the nation's top female collegiate basketball player. She also was named a Kodak All-American and selected to the NCAA Women's Basketball Team of the Decade for the 1980s.

International Basketball

Throughout her college career, Weatherspoon also played international basketball as a member of the U.S. Women's Basketball Team. She helped the team win the Women's Basketball World Championship in 1986 and claim gold medals at both the Goodwill Games and World University Games in 1987. After graduating from college, Weatherspoon was a member of the U.S. Women's Olympic basketball team that won a gold medal at the 1988 Olympic Games in Seoul, South Korea.

After winning the gold medal, Weatherspoon and her Olympic teammates found their options for a basketball career limited. Since no women's professional league existed in the United States at that time, she and several

Weatherspoon (8) defends against Irina Minkh of the Soviet Union in the 1988 Summer Olympics. The United States won the game 102-88 to advance to the gold medal round.

other top players decided to join pro teams in Europe. Weatherspoon spent six years in Italy playing for three different teams—Busto, Magenta, and Como. She also spent two years in Russia playing for CSKA. "In 1993 I was among the first Americans ever to play pro ball in Russia. And boy, it sure was a challenge," she remembered. "We had come on the heels of an uneasy political relationship between the United States and Russia. No one spoke English on my team, and I didn't know Russian. We used sign language to communicate."

Weatherspoon took time out from her European professional leagues to play in the Olympics once again in 1992, when the American team claimed a bronze medal. "I don't think that what winning the gold medal really meant hit me until 1992," she noted. "When we won the bronze that year, I dropped my head and walked away. I didn't even want to touch that bronze medal. I saw the bronze as a prize for being a failure. But then I realized that when I walked away with my head down, I embarrassed myself. I understood that the Olympics are about more than winning it all. They're about competing, playing for your country. . . . Now I cherish the bronze medal as much as the gold medal."

"There is no other place for my personality than New York. No other place. This is home," Weatherspoon said. "It fits me. It fits the way I like to take on challenges. And New York is definitely a challenge."

WNBA—The New York Liberty

Throughout her years overseas, Weatherspoon always hoped to have the opportunity to play professional basketball in the United States someday "The whole time I'm daydreaming," she recalled. "I'm saying to myself, 'I wish they could see me now . . . see what I can do now.'" She finally got her chance in 1997, when the Women's National Basketball Association (WNBA) was formed. Unlike earlier women's leagues that quickly failed, this league had the financial backing of the men's league, the National Basketball Association (NBA). WNBA games were scheduled to take place in the summer, which was the NBA's off-season.

Shortly after the WNBA was formed, Weatherspoon signed a contract to play for the New York Liberty. "There is no other place for my personality than New York. No other place. This is home," she said. "It fits me. It fits the way I like to take on challenges. And New York is definitely a challenge." Weatherspoon proved that she fit in on her first day in New York

Weatherspoon drives to the basket against the Houston Comets in the 1997 WNBA Championship game.

City. While touring Manhattan on a double-decker bus, she and her teammates stopped at a park to have their picture taken with the Statue of Liberty in the background. Noticing a police boat along the shore, Weatherspoon went over and introduced herself to the crew, who turned out to be basketball fans. She convinced the officers not only to take her for a ride, but to let her drive the boat around the harbor while her teammates cheered from shore.

In the first game in WNBA history, the Liberty defeated the Los Angeles Sparks, 67-57. The Liberty used this historic victory as a launching pad for a highly successful inaugural season. Spurred on by Weatherspoon's tenacious defense, pinpoint passes, and boundless energy, New York finished the inaugural season with a 17-11 record and advanced to the WNBA finals. The Liberty's bid for the first-ever WNBA title fell short, though, when the team lost the championship series to the Houston Comets.

By season's end, Weatherspoon was recognized as one of the best players in the new league. She led the WNBA in steals (with 3.04 per game) and assists (with 6.1 per game) and added 7 points a game as well. She was named the WNBA's Defensive Player of the Year and made the All-WNBA Second Team. "She may be the best guard who has ever played this game," said Liberty Coach Carol Blazejowski. "There's no question that she's the heart and soul of our team."

Weatherspoon had another great year in 1998. She led the league in steals once again (with 3.33 per game), ranked second in assists (with 2.4), and added 6.8 points per game. She was named WNBA Defensive Player of the Year for the second consecutive time and also made the All-WNBA Second Team. Unfortunately, the Liberty missed the playoffs by one game.

Most Famous Shot in WNBA History

In the 1999 season, Weatherspoon averaged 7.2 points, 6.4 assists, and 2.44 steals per game, ranking second in the league in the latter two categories. Her strong performance helped ensure her selection to the first-ever WNBA All-Star Game. The Liberty posted an 18-14 record, won the Eastern Conference, and advanced through the playoffs to the WNBA Finals. New York lost the first game of the best-of-three championship series to the Houston Comets and faced elimination in Game 2. But Weatherspoon tied the series for her team with one of the most famous shots in WNBA history.

Trailing by two points with 2.4 seconds remaining, the Liberty took the ball inbounds. Comets fans were so certain of their team's victory that confetti had already begun falling from the rafters. But Weatherspoon caught the inbounds pass, took a couple of dribbles, and threw the ball toward the basket from beyond halfcourt. "I wasn't going to look for anyone. I was going to live or die with that shot. I didn't want any of my teammates to have to live with missing that shot during the off-season. If it didn't go in, I wanted to be the one to have to live with that," she explained. "It felt pretty good when it left my hands. I was just praying that it went in and that we'd have a chance for Game 3."

Weatherspoon (11) and Sheryl Swoopes (22) of the Houston Comets battle for possession of a loose ball in 1999 action.

The shot banked off the backboard and dropped through the hoop as the buzzer sounded, giving the Liberty a 68-67 victory and tying the series at 1-1. As the crowd grew silent with shock, Weatherspoon fell to the floor and was buried by her joyous teammates. Even though New York lost Game 3, Weatherspoon's last-second heroics have been featured in numerous WNBA commercials in the years since. "What puts it to the side a little bit is that we didn't win the championship," she noted. "But it was good for the league."

By the time the 1999 season ended, Weatherspoon had reached the peak of her fame. She was the most popular player on the Liberty, and her number 11 jersey (chosen to honor a favorite uncle who passed away when she was 11 years old) ranked among the best sellers for men or women at the NBA Store in Manhattan. Her energetic play helped the Liberty draw an average of 13,000 fans to Madison Square Garden for home games and attract two million viewers for televised games.

Weatherspoon chose this time to publish a book, *Teresa Weatherspoon's Basketball for Girls*. Aimed at school-age girls, it provides detailed instructions on all aspects of the game. It also includes numerous sidebars in which Weatherspoon shares her own thoughts and experiences as a basketball player. "The personal anecdotes and up-to-date photographs make this title especially appealing," wrote Barb Lawler in a review for *School Library Journal*. "An excellent resource for sports collections." "A must for any girl with a serious interest in playing the sport, this will also be good reading for basketball fans in general," added Helen Rosenberg in *Booklist*.

Working to Stay on Top

During the 2000 season, the Liberty went 20-12 to win the Eastern Conference. They advanced to the WNBA Finals for the third time, but they lost to the Houston Comets once again. Weatherspoon had another solid season, averaging 6.4 points, 6.4 assists, and 2.03 steals per game. She started for the Eastern Conference in the All-Star Game and was named to the All-WNBA Second Team for the fourth consecutive year.

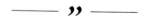

"Let me say, for the record, I have not said anything about retirement. . . . I feel great at my age. To me, age is just a number. It's a matter of how you take care of yourself."

In 2001 the Liberty posted a franchise-best 21-11 record but were eliminated from the playoffs in the Eastern Conference finals. Weatherspoon averaged 6.5 points, 6.3 assists, and 1.72 steals per game and started in the All-Star Game for the third straight year. But she was slowed by a pulled hamstring late in the season, and her struggles in the closing weeks led some people to wonder whether she had lost a step compared to her prime playing days. In fact, some critics questioned whether, at age 30, she could defend younger, quicker guards like Sue Bird of the Seattle Storm. "I've heard what they've said. The only talk that matters to me is what my teammates say. Spoon is still here," she responded. "Let me say, for the record, I have not said anything about retirement. . . . I feel great at my age. To me, age is just a number. It's a matter of how you take care of yourself."

Teammates also have noted that critics sometimes fail to appreciate Weatherspoon's role as the emotional center of her team. "We have a leader in Teresa Weatherspoon," said her teammate Sophia Witherspoon. "She brings such aggressiveness and excitement. She has a winning spirit and a

143

big heart. She hates to lose." Or as another teammate, Kym Hampton, noted: "If she can't get you pepped up, you're probably dead." Indeed, Weatherspoon could always be counted on to dive for loose balls, distribute behind-the-back and no-look passes, and bring the crowd to its feet with "raise the roof" gestures. "When I'm playing and jumping and hollering, I want to pull everybody in," she explained. "Feel what I feel. Feel the joy of this game — the joy of having some sort of passion for what you do. When I look up there and see those kids jumping and screaming, I know they're feeling it. That's a tremendous joy."

"When I'm playing and jumping and hollering, I want to pull everybody in," Weatherspoon explained. "Feel the joy of this game — the joy of having some sort of passion for what you do. When I look up there and see those kids jumping and screaming, I know they're feeling it. That's a tremendous joy."

Reaching Historic Milestones

In 2002 Weatherspoon's production dipped to 3.4 points and 1.31 steals per game, although her assist average (5.7 per game) ranked third in the league. She also became the first player in WNBA history to record 1,000 points and 1,000 assists in her career, and she made the All-Star Team for the fourth straight year. The Liberty advanced to the WNBA Finals for the fourth time in six years, but they were disappointed yet again. This time, however, it was the Los Angeles Sparks rather than the Houston Comets that eliminated New York.

Weatherspoon started to see a reduction in her floor time in 2003, as her minutes played per game fell from 30 to 24. Consequently, her production declined to 2.9 points, 4.4 assists, and .82 steals per contest. She was selected to the All-Star Team for a fifth time, but the Liberty failed to make the playoffs by one game.

At the conclusion of the season, team management decided to make major changes to the Liberty lineup. In order to rebuild the franchise with younger players, they did not renew the contracts of Weatherspoon and six other veterans. Liberty management offered Weatherspoon a position in the front office if she agreed to retire, but she decided to test the free-agent market instead. "I don't know if disappointment is the word to describe how I felt when I was told that the Liberty were not going to offer me a new contract," she stated. "I was crushed and hurt. I loved playing in

Weatherspoon emerged as one of the first true stars of the WNBA during her years with the New York Liberty.

Weatherspoon, shown here shaking hands with kids before the 2003 WNBA All-Star Game, has been a tireless ambassador for women's basketball.

New York, in Madison Square Garden, and I built such great friendships with so many people there. It's the relationships that I developed with the youth of the city that I am going to truly miss."

A New Challenge

Determined to win a WNBA championship before calling it quits, Weatherspoon signed a contract with the Los Angeles Sparks, a loaded squad that had won the WNBA title in 2002 and nearly repeated as champs in 2003. Although she expressed disappointment at not finishing her career in New York, Weatherspoon was delighted to join such a high-caliber team. "I was taught that when you move on you don't look back or you run into something. And when a potential championship team offers you a chance to play, well, you can't be stupid," she stated. "I now have the opportunity to play with such incredible players. I keep asking myself, 'With all of these talented players, who am I going to pass the ball to when we run the break?'"

The Sparks hoped that Weatherspoon's defensive abilities and leadership would help the team return to the top of the WNBA. "I'm very happy to acquire a player of Teresa's character," said Sparks Coach Michael Cooper.

"She is a defensive-minded person and defense wins championships. We're blessed with a good core group, so it's about adding pieces. And Teresa is an important piece."

As the 2004 season got underway, Weatherspoon came off the bench for the first time in her long career. In fact, through the end of the 2003 season she had started 220 consecutive WNBA games—or every game her team had played since the league was founded. She averaged only 8 minutes per game for the Sparks, and her production declined accordingly. Still, Weatherspoon was seen as a valuable asset in the Sparks' quest for another WNBA crown. Unfortunately, the team was knocked out of contention by Sacramento, 73-58, and eliminated in the first round.

A Lasting Legacy

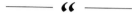

Weatherspoon is the WNBA's all-time assist leader, with a career total of 1,338 through the 2004 season. She also has 465 career steals and 1,264 points. As she nears the age of 40, she still loves the game of basketball as much as she did when she was four. "Basketball is like food to me. I can't survive without it," she stated. "I get emotional even when I think of stepping inside those four lines, and I think, 'Now it's my turn to show you my talents. Now it's my turn to entertain.' And when those 40 minutes are

"The future of women's basketball and the WNBA in this country is going to be huge. You have younger ladies now able to see what they can be by watching what's happening with us."

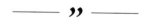

done, I can't wait till the next time. I love to go to practice, too. I play and I practice like I'll never play or practice again. When I walk away, I'm beat. I'm dead tired. This game means so much to me."

Weatherspoon also enjoys sharing her love of basketball with others. She signs endless autographs for fans, appears at camps and clinics, and speaks at schools. "I've always said to kids, 'Persist until you succeed,'" she related. "Because a lot of times when obstacles are in front of them and they don't seem as if they can remove it, they tend to stop. But if they persist until they succeed, that's when they will be very proud of their accomplishments."

Weatherspoon is a tireless promoter of women's basketball. She believes that the women's game is just as good as the men's—and is poised to get better. "I want to be accepted not as a 'female athlete' but as an athlete. We're gaining respect, but I want people to understand that we play this game just as hard as men do," she noted. "The future of women's basketball and the WNBA in this country is going to be huge. You have younger ladies now able to see what they can be by watching what's happening with us. They can see the emotion that we play with, the enthusiasm, the love, the joy that we have playing the game here in America. That emotion, joy, and enthusiasm is trickling down to them. Now they're just waiting for their turn. That's why I think it's going to be even greater as the years go on."

HOME AND FAMILY

Weatherspoon, who is single, lives in Los Angeles during the WNBA season. In the off-season she returns to her hometown of Pineland, Texas, to be near her family—and especially her mother. "My mother is a warrior, a true warrior, and that's the way I am when I play the game," she noted. "I dedicate basically everything I do to my mother, because she made me who I am."

HOBBIES AND OTHER INTERESTS

In her spare time, Weatherspoon enjoys going bowling, playing tennis, and reading. She is also active in charity work for the Women's Sports Foundation, anti-drug campaigns, and children's basketball camps.

WRITINGS

Teresa Weatherspoon's Basketball for Girls, 1999 (with Tara Sullivan and Kelly Whiteside)

AWARDS AND HONORS

Women's Basketball World Championships: 1986, gold medal
Goodwill Games, Women's Basketball: 1986, gold medal
World University Games, Women's Basketball: 1987, gold medal
Kodak NCAA All-American: 1987, 1988
NCAA Women's Basketball Championship: 1988
Wade Trophy: 1988
Broderick Cup: 1988
Olympic Women's Basketball: 1988, gold medal; 1992, bronze medal
NCAA Women's Basketball Team of the Decade: 1980s
WNBA Defensive Player of the Year: 1997, 1998
All-WNBA Second Team: 1997, 1998, 1999, 2000
WNBA All-Star Team: 1999, 2000, 2001, 2002, 2003

FURTHER READING

Books

Ponti, James. *WNBA: Stars of Women's Basketball*, 1999
Weatherspoon, Teresa, with Tara Sullivan and Kelly Whiteside. *Teresa Weatherspoon's Basketball for Girls*, 1999
Who's Who among African Americans, 2004

Periodicals

Los Angeles Times, Feb. 5, 2004, Sports, p.8
New York Daily News, June 19, 1997, p.86; June 30, 1998, p.57
New York Times, July 14, 1997, p.C7; Sep. 5, 1999, Sports, p.1; Aug. 9, 2000, p.D1; June 2, 2002, Sports, p.4; May 21, 2004, p.D8
New Yorker, Aug. 16, 1999, p.36
Sports Illustrated, Apr. 11, 1988, p.40; July 14, 1997, p.50
Sports Illustrated for Kids, July 1998, p.52
Sports Illustrated for Women, Nov. 2001, p.77
Women's Sports and Fitness, June 1988, p.46

Online Articles

http://www.wbmagazine.com
(*Women's Basketball Magazine*, "Weatherspoon Sparks," 2004)

Online Databases

Biography Resource Center, 2004, article from *Who's Who among African Americans*, 2004
Current Biography Electronic, 2000

ADDRESS

Teresa Weatherspoon
Los Angeles Sparks
555 N. Nash St.
El Segundo, CA 90245

WORLD WIDE WEB SITE

http://www.wnba.com

Photo and Illustration Credits

Freddy Adu/Photos: AP/Wide World Photos; Stan Honda/AFP/Getty Images (p. 13); AP/Wide World Photos; Jamie Squire/Getty Images (p. 20).

Tina Basich/Photos: Michael Germana/UPI/Landov; Nate Christenson (pp. 27, 30); Justine Chiara. Cover: PRETTY GOOD FOR A GIRL (HarperCollins Publishers) copyright © 2003 by Tina Basich with Kathleen Gasperini.

Sasha Cohen/Photos: AP/Wide World Photos; Mike Powell/Getty Images (p. 45).

Dale Earnhardt, Jr./Photos: AP/Wide World Photos.

LeBron James/Photos: Nathaniel S. Butler/NBAE/Getty Images; Tom Pidgeon/Getty Images (p. 76); AP/Wide World Photos.

Carly Patterson/Photos: AP/Wide World Photos.

Albert Pujols/Photos: AP/Wide World Photos

Michael Strahan/Photos: Kimberly Butler/Time Life Pictures/Getty Images; Stephen Dunn/Getty Images; AP/Wide World Photos; Getty Images; AP/Wide World Photos.

Teresa Weatherspoon/Photos: Andrew D. Bernstein/NBAE/Getty Images; Louisiana Tech Media Relations; AP/Wide World Photos; Doug Pensinger/Getty Images; AP/Wide World Photos; Rocky Widner/WNBAE/Getty Images; AP/Wide World Photos.

How to Use the Cumulative Index

Our indexes have a new look. In an effort to make our indexes easier to use, we've combined the Name and General Index into a new, Cumulative Index. This single ready-reference resource covers all the volumes in *Biography Today*, both the general series and the special subject series. The new Cumulative Index contains complete listings of all individuals who have appeared in *Biography Today* since the series began. Their names appear in bold-faced type, followed by the issue in which they appear. The Cumulative Index also includes references for the occupations, nationalities, and ethnic and minority origins of individuals profiled in *Biography Today*.

We have also made some changes to our specialty indexes, the Places of Birth Index and the Birthday Index. To consolidate and to save space, the Places of Birth Index and the Birthday Index will no longer appear in the January and April issues of the softbound subscription series. But these indexes can still be found in the September issue of the softbound subscription series, in the hardbound Annual Cumulation at the end of each year, and in each volume of the special subject series.

General Series

The General Series of *Biography Today* is denoted in the index with the month and year of the issue in which the individual appeared. Each individual also appears in the Annual Cumulation for that year.

Special Subject Series

The Special Subject Series of *Biography Today* are each denoted in the index with an abbreviated form of the series name, plus the number of the volume in which the individual appears. They are listed as follows.

Updates

Updated information on selected individuals appears in the Appendix at the end of some issues of the *Biography Today* Annual Cumulation. In the index, the original entry is listed first, followed by any updates.

Cumulative Index

This cumulative index includes names, occupations, nationalities, and ethnic and minority origins that pertain to all individuals profiled in *Biography Today* since the debut of the series in 1992.

171

Places of Birth Index

The following index lists the places of birth for the individuals profiled in *Biography Today*. Places of birth are entered under state, province, and/or country.

Yep, Laurence – *San Francisco* . . Author V.5

Canada

Blanchard, Rachel – *Toronto, Ontario* Apr 97
Campbell, Neve – *Toronto, Ontario* . . Apr 98
Candy, John – *Newmarket, Ontario* . . Sep 94
Carrey, Jim – *Newmarket, Ontario* . . . Apr 96
Dion, Celine – *Charlemagne, Quebec* . Sep 97
Giguère, Jean-Sébastien – *Montreal,*
  Quebec. . . . . Sport V.10
Gretzky, Wayne – *Brantford, Ontario* Jan 92
Howe, Gordie – *Floral,*
  Saskatchewan . . . . Sport V.2
Jennings, Peter – *Toronto, Ontario.* . . . Jul 92
Johnston, Lynn – *Collingwood,*
  Ontario. . . . . Jan 99
Kielburger, Craig – *Toronto, Ontario* . . Jan 00
lang, k.d. – *Edmonton, Alberta* . . . . . . Sep 93
Lavigne, Avril – *Belleville,*
  Ontario . . . . PerfArt V.2
Lemieux, Mario – *Montreal, Quebec* . . Jul 92
Martin, Bernard – *Petty Harbor,*
  Newfoundland . . . . WorLdr V.3
Messier, Mark – *Edmonton, Alberta* . . Apr 96
Morissette, Alanis – *Ottawa, Ontario* Apr 97
Mowat, Farley – *Belleville,*
  Ontario. . . . . Author V.8
Myers, Mike – *Toronto, Ontario.* . PerfArt V.3
Priestley, Jason – *Vancouver,*
  British Columbia . . . . Apr 92
Roy, Patrick – *Quebec City,*
  Quebec. . . . . Sport V.7
Sakic, Joe – *Burnbary,*
  British Columbia. . . . . Sport V.6
Shatner, William – *Montreal, Quebec* Apr 95
Twain, Shania – *Windsor, Ontario.* . . . Apr 99
Vernon, Mike – *Calgary, Alberta.* . . . . Jan 98
Watson, Paul – *Toronto, Ontario.* . WorLdr V.1
Wolf, Hazel – *Victoria,*
  British Columbia . . . . WorLdr V.3
Yzerman, Steve – *Cranbrook,*
  British Columbia. . . . . Sport V.2

China

Chan, Jackie – *Hong Kong.* . . . . . . PerfArt V.1
Dai Qing – *Chongqing* . . . . WorLdr V.3
Fu Mingxia – *Wuhan* . . . . Sport V.5
Lucid, Shannon – *Shanghai.* . . . Science V.2
Paterson, Katherine – *Qing Jiang,*
  Jiangsu . . . . Author 97
Pei, I.M. – *Canton* . . . . Artist V.1
Wang, An – *Shanghai* . . . . Science V.2
Yao Ming – *Shanghai* . . . . Sep 03
Yuen Wo-Ping – *Guangzhou* . . . PerfArt V.3

Colombia

Ocampo, Adriana C.
  – *Barranquilla.* . . . . Science V.8
Shakira – *Barranquilla.* . . . . PerfArt V.1

Colorado

Allen, Tim – *Denver* . . . . Apr 94
Bryan, Zachery Ty – *Aurora* . . . . Jan 97
Dunlap, Alison – *Denver* . . . . Sport V.7
Handler, Ruth – *Denver* . . . . Apr 98
Klug, Chris – *Vail* . . . . Sport V.8
Patterson, Ryan – *Grand*
  Junction . . . . Science V.7
Romero, John
  – *Colorado Springs* . . . . Science V.8
Stachowski, Richie – *Denver.* . . . Science V.3
Toro, Natalia – *Boulder* . . . . Sep 99
Van Dyken, Amy – *Englewood* . . . Sport V.3

Connecticut

Brandis, Jonathan – *Danbury* . . . . Sep 95
Bush, George W. – *New Haven* . . . . . Sep 00
Cantore, Jim – *Waterbury.* . . . . . . Science V.9
dePaola, Tomie – *Meriden* . . . . . Author V.5
Land, Edwin – *Bridgeport* . . . . . . Science V.1
Leibovitz, Annie – *Waterbury* . . . . . . Sep 96
Lobo, Rebecca – *Hartford* . . . . Sport V.3
Mayer, John – *Bridgeport* . . . . Apr 04
McClintock, Barbara – *Hartford.* . . . . Oct 92
Shea, Jim, Jr. – *Hartford* . . . . Sport V.8
Spelman, Lucy – *Bridgeport* . . . . Science V.6
Spock, Benjamin – *New Haven* . . . . . Sep 95
Tarbox, Katie – *New Canaan* . . . Author V.10

Cuba

Castro, Fidel – *Mayari, Oriente* . . . . . . Jul 92
Cruz, Celia –*Havana.* . . . . Apr 04
Estefan, Gloria – *Havana* . . . . Jul 92
Fuentes, Daisy – *Havana.* . . . . Jan 94
Hernandez, Livan – *Villa Clara* . . . . . Apr 98
Zamora, Pedro . . . . Apr 95

Czechoslovakia

Albright, Madeleine – *Prague* . . . . . . Apr 97
Hasek, Dominik – *Pardubice* . . . . . Sport V.3
Hingis, Martina – *Kosice* . . . . Sport V.2
Jagr, Jaromir – *Kladno.* . . . . Sport V.5
Navratilova, Martina – *Prague* . . . . . . Jan 93

Delaware

Heimlich, Henry – *Wilmington* . . Science V.6

Dominican Republic

Martinez, Pedro – *Manoguayabo.* . Sport V.5
Pujols, Albert – *Santo Domingo* . . Sport V.12
Soriano, Alfonso
  – *San Pedro de Macoris* . . . . Sport V.10

New Zealand

Nigeria

North Carolina

Birthday Index

Biography Today

General Series

Biography Today **General Series** includes a unique combination of current biographical profiles that teachers and librarians — and the readers themselves — tell us are most appealing. The **General Series** is available as a 3-issue subscription; hardcover annual cumulation; or subscription plus cumulation.

Within the **General Series**, your readers will find a variety of sketches about:

- Authors
- Musicians
- Political leaders
- Sports figures
- Movie actresses & actors
- Cartoonists
- Scientists
- Astronauts
- TV personalities
- and the movers & shakers in many other fields!

"Biography Today will be useful in elementary and middle school libraries and in public library children's collections where there is a need for biographies of current personalities. High schools serving reluctant readers may also want to consider a subscription."
— *Booklist,* American Library Association

"Highly recommended for the young adult audience. Readers will delight in the accessible, energetic, tell-all style; teachers, librarians, and parents will welcome the clever format, intelligent and informative text. It should prove especially useful in motivating 'reluctant' readers or literate nonreaders."
— *MultiCultural Review*

"Written in a friendly, almost chatty tone, the profiles offer quick, objective information. While coverage of current figures makes *Biography Today* a useful reference tool, an appealing format and wide scope make it a fun resource to browse." — *School Library Journal*

"The best source for current information at a level kids can understand."
— Kelly Bryant, School Librarian, Carlton, OR

"Easy for kids to read. We love it! Don't want to be without it."
— Lynn McWhirter, School Librarian, Rockford, IL

ONE-YEAR SUBSCRIPTION
- 3 softcover issues, 6" x 9"
- Published in January, April, and September
- 1-year subscription, $60
- 150 pages per issue
- 10 profiles per issue
- Contact sources for additional information
- Cumulative General, Places of Birth, and Birthday Indexes

HARDBOUND ANNUAL CUMULATION
- Sturdy 6" x 9" hardbound volume
- Published in December
- $62 per volume
- 450 pages per volume
- 25-30 profiles — includes all profiles found in softcover issues for that calendar year
- Cumulative General, Places of Birth, and Birthday Indexes
- Special appendix features current updates of previous profiles

SUBSCRIPTION AND CUMULATION COMBINATION
- $99 for 3 softcover issues plus the hardbound volume

1992

Paula Abdul
Andre Agassi
Kirstie Alley
Terry Anderson
Roseanne Arnold
Isaac Asimov
James Baker
Charles Barkley
Larry Bird
Judy Blume
Berke Breathed
Garth Brooks
Barbara Bush
George Bush
Fidel Castro
Bill Clinton
Bill Cosby
Diana, Princess of Wales
Shannen Doherty
Elizabeth Dole
David Duke
Gloria Estefan
Mikhail Gorbachev
Steffi Graf
Wayne Gretzky
Matt Groening
Alex Haley
Hammer
Martin Handford
Stephen Hawking
Hulk Hogan
Saddam Hussein
Lee Iacocca
Bo Jackson
Mae Jemison
Peter Jennings
Steven Jobs
Pope John Paul II
Magic Johnson
Michael Jordon
Jackie Joyner-Kersee
Spike Lee
Mario Lemieux
Madeleine L'Engle
Jay Leno
Yo-Yo Ma
Nelson Mandela
Wynton Marsalis
Thurgood Marshall
Ann Martin
Barbara McClintock
Emily Arnold McCully
Antonia Novello

Sandra Day O'Connor
Rosa Parks
Jane Pauley
H. Ross Perot
Luke Perry
Scottie Pippen
Colin Powell
Jason Priestley
Queen Latifah
Yitzhak Rabin
Sally Ride
Pete Rose
Nolan Ryan
H. Norman
    Schwarzkopf
Jerry Seinfeld
Dr. Seuss
Gloria Steinem
Clarence Thomas
Chris Van Allsburg
Cynthia Voigt
Bill Watterson
Robin Williams
Oprah Winfrey
Kristi Yamaguchi
Boris Yeltsin

1993

Maya Angelou
Arthur Ashe
Avi
Kathleen Battle
Candice Bergen
Boutros Boutros-Ghali
Chris Burke
Dana Carvey
Cesar Chavez
Henry Cisneros
Hillary Rodham Clinton
Jacques Cousteau
Cindy Crawford
Macaulay Culkin
Lois Duncan
Marian Wright Edelman
Cecil Fielder
Bill Gates
Sara Gilbert
Dizzy Gillespie
Al Gore
Cathy Guisewite
Jasmine Guy
Anita Hill
Ice-T
Darci Kistler

k.d. lang
Dan Marino
Rigoberta Menchu
Walter Dean Myers
Martina Navratilova
Phyllis Reynolds Naylor
Rudolf Nureyev
Shaquille O'Neal
Janet Reno
Jerry Rice
Mary Robinson
Winona Ryder
Jerry Spinelli
Denzel Washington
Keenen Ivory Wayans
Dave Winfield

1994

Tim Allen
Marian Anderson
Mario Andretti
Ned Andrews
Yasir Arafat
Bruce Babbitt
Mayim Bialik
Bonnie Blair
Ed Bradley
John Candy
Mary Chapin Carpenter
Benjamin Chavis
Connie Chung
Beverly Cleary
Kurt Cobain
F.W. de Klerk
Rita Dove
Linda Ellerbee
Sergei Fedorov
Zlata Filipovic
Daisy Fuentes
Ruth Bader Ginsburg
Whoopi Goldberg
Tonya Harding
Melissa Joan Hart
Geoff Hooper
Whitney Houston
Dan Jansen
Nancy Kerrigan
Alexi Lalas
Charlotte Lopez
Wilma Mankiller
Shannon Miller
Toni Morrison
Richard Nixon
Greg Norman
Severo Ochoa

River Phoenix
Elizabeth Pine
Jonas Salk
Richard Scarry
Emmitt Smith
Will Smith
Steven Spielberg
Patrick Stewart
R.L. Stine
Lewis Thomas
Barbara Walters
Charlie Ward
Steve Young
Kim Zmeskal

1995

Troy Aikman
Jean-Bertrand Aristide
Oksana Baiul
Halle Berry
Benazir Bhutto
Jonathan Brandis
Warren E. Burger
Ken Burns
Candace Cameron
Jimmy Carter
Agnes de Mille
Placido Domingo
Janet Evans
Patrick Ewing
Newt Gingrich
John Goodman
Amy Grant
Jesse Jackson
James Earl Jones
Julie Krone
David Letterman
Rush Limbaugh
Heather Locklear
Reba McEntire
Joe Montana
Cosmas Ndeti
Hakeem Olajuwon
Ashley Olsen
Mary-Kate Olsen
Jennifer Parkinson
Linus Pauling
Itzhak Perlman
Cokie Roberts
Wilma Rudolph
Salt 'N' Pepa
Barry Sanders
William Shatner
Elizabeth George
    Speare

Dr. Benjamin Spock
Jonathan Taylor
    Thomas
Vicki Van Meter
Heather Whitestone
Pedro Zamora

1996

Aung San Suu Kyi
Boyz II Men
Brandy
Ron Brown
Mariah Carey
Jim Carrey
Larry Champagne III
Christo
Chelsea Clinton
Coolio
Bob Dole
David Duchovny
Debbi Fields
Chris Galeczka
Jerry Garcia
Jennie Garth
Wendy Guey
Tom Hanks
Alison Hargreaves
Sir Edmund Hillary
Judith Jamison
Barbara Jordan
Annie Leibovitz
Carl Lewis
Jim Lovell
Mickey Mantle
Lynn Margulis
Iqbal Masih
Mark Messier
Larisa Oleynik
Christopher Pike
David Robinson
Dennis Rodman
Selena
Monica Seles
Don Shula
Kerri Strug
Tiffani-Amber Thiessen
Dave Thomas
Jaleel White

1997

Madeleine Albright
Marcus Allen
Gillian Anderson
Rachel Blanchard
Zachery Ty Bryan
Adam Ezra Cohen
Claire Danes
Celine Dion
Jean Driscoll
Louis Farrakhan
Ella Fitzgerald
Harrison Ford
Bryant Gumbel
John Johnson
Michael Johnson
Maya Lin
George Lucas
John Madden
Bill Monroe
Alanis Morissette
Sam Morrison
Rosie O'Donnell
Muammar el-Qaddafi
Christopher Reeve
Pete Sampras
Pat Schroeder
Rebecca Sealfon
Tupac Shakur
Tabitha Soren
Herbert Tarvin
Merlin Tuttle
Mara Wilson

1998

Bella Abzug
Kofi Annan
Neve Campbell
Sean Combs (Puff
    Daddy)
Dalai Lama (Tenzin
    Gyatso)
Diana, Princess of Wales
Leonardo DiCaprio
Walter E. Diemer
Ruth Handler
Hanson
Livan Hernandez
Jewel
Jimmy Johnson
Tara Lipinski
Jody-Anne Maxwell
Dominique Moceanu
Alexandra Nechita

Brad Pitt
LeAnn Rimes
Emily Rosa
David Satcher
Betty Shabazz
Kordell Stewart
Shinichi Suzuki
Mother Teresa
Mike Vernon
Reggie White
Kate Winslet

1999

Ben Affleck
Jennifer Aniston
Maurice Ashley
Kobe Bryant
Bessie Delany
Sadie Delany
Sharon Draper
Sarah Michelle Gellar
John Glenn
Savion Glover
Jeff Gordon
David Hampton
Lauryn Hill
King Hussein
Lynn Johnston
Shari Lewis
Oseola McCarty
Mark McGwire
Slobodan Milosevic
Natalie Portman
J. K. Rowling
Frank Sinatra
Gene Siskel
Sammy Sosa
John Stanford
Natalia Toro
Shania Twain
Mitsuko Uchida
Jesse Ventura
Venus Williams

2000

Christina Aguilera
K.A. Applegate
Lance Armstrong
Backstreet Boys
Daisy Bates
Harry Blackmun
George W. Bush
Carson Daly
Ron Dayne
Henry Louis Gates, Jr.
Doris Haddock
    (Granny D)
Jennifer Love Hewitt
Chamique Holdsclaw
Katie Holmes
Charlayne Hunter-Gault
Johanna Johnson
Craig Kielburger
John Lasseter
Peyton Manning
Ricky Martin
John McCain
Walter Payton
Freddie Prinze, Jr.
Viviana Risca
Briana Scurry
George Thampy
CeCe Winans

2001

Jessica Alba
Christiane Amanpour
Drew Barrymore
Jeff Bezos
Destiny's Child
Dale Earnhardt
Carly Fiorina
Aretha Franklin
Cathy Freeman
Tony Hawk
Faith Hill
Kim Dae-jung
Madeleine L'Engle
Mariangela Lisanti
Frankie Muniz
*N Sync
Ellen Ochoa
Jeff Probst
Julia Roberts
Carl T. Rowan
Britney Spears
Chris Tucker
Lloyd D. Ward
Alan Webb
Chris Weinke

2002

Aaliyah
Osama bin Laden
Mary J. Blige
Aubyn Burnside
Aaron Carter
Julz Chavez
Dick Cheney
Hilary Duff
Billy Gilman
Rudolph Giuliani
Brian Griese
Jennifer Lopez
Dave Mirra
Dineh Mohajer
Leanne Nakamura
Daniel Radcliffe
Condoleezza Rice
Marla Runyan
Ruth Simmons
Mattie Stepanek
J.R.R. Tolkien
Barry Watson
Tyrone Willingham
Elijah Wood

2003

Yolanda Adams
Olivia Bennett
Mildred Benson
Alexis Bledel
Barry Bonds
Vincent Brooks
Laura Bush
Amanda Bynes
Kelly Clarkson
Vin Diesel
Eminem
Michele Forman
Vicente Fox
Millard Fuller
Josh Hartnett
Dolores Huerta

Sarah Hughes
Enrique Iglesias
Jeanette Lee
John Lewis
Nicklas Lidstrom
Clint Mathis
Donovan McNabb
Nelly
Andy Roddick
Gwen Stefani
Emma Watson
Meg Whitman
Reese Witherspoon
Yao Ming

2004

Natalie Babbitt
David Beckham
Francie Berger
Tony Blair
Orlando Bloom
Kim Clijsters
Celia Cruz
Matel Dawson, Jr.
The Donnas
Tim Duncan
Shirin Ebadi
Carla Hayden
Ashton Kutcher
Lisa Leslie
Linkin Park
Lindsay Lohan
Irene D. Long
John Mayer
Mandy Moore
Thich Nhat Hanh
OutKast
Raven
Ronald Reagan
Keanu Reeves
Ricardo Sanchez
Brian Urlacher
Alexa Vega
Michelle Wie
Will Wright

Biography Today

Subject Series

For ages 9 and above

Expands and complements the General Series and targets specific subject areas . . .

Our readers asked for it! They wanted more biographies, and the *Biography Today* **Subject Series** is our response to that demand. Now your readers can choose their special areas of interest and go on to read about their favorites in those fields. Priced at just $39 per volume, the following specific volumes are included in the *Biography Today* **Subject Series**:

- **Authors**
- **Business Leaders**
- **Performing Artists**
- **Scientists & Inventors**
- **Sports**

FEATURES AND FORMAT

- Sturdy 6" x 9" hardbound volumes
- Individual volumes, $39 each
- 200 pages per volume
- 10 profiles per volume — targets individuals within a specific subject area
- Contact sources for additional information
- Cumulative General, Places of Birth, and Birthday Indexes

NOTE: There is *no duplication of entries* between the **General Series** of *Biography Today* and the **Subject Series**.

AUTHORS

"A useful tool for children's assignment needs." — *School Library Journal*

"The prose is workmanlike: report writers will find enough detail to begin sound investigations, and browsers are likely to find someone of interest." — *School Library Journal*

SCIENTISTS & INVENTORS

"The articles are readable, attractively laid out, and touch on important points that will suit assignment needs. Browsers will note the clear writing and interesting details." — *School Library Journal*

"The book is excellent for demonstrating that scientists are real people with widely diverse backgrounds and personal interests. The biographies are fascinating to read." — *The Science Teacher*

SPORTS

"This series should become a standard resource in libraries that serve intermediate students." — *School Library Journal*

Authors

VOLUME 1

Eric Carle
Alice Childress
Robert Cormier
Roald Dahl
Jim Davis
John Grisham
Virginia Hamilton
James Herriot
S.E. Hinton
M.E. Kerr
Stephen King
Gary Larson
Joan Lowery Nixon
Gary Paulsen
Cynthia Rylant
Mildred D. Taylor
Kurt Vonnegut, Jr.
E.B. White
Paul Zindel

VOLUME 2

James Baldwin
Stan and Jan Berenstain
David Macaulay
Patricia MacLachlan
Scott O'Dell
Jerry Pinkney
Jack Prelutsky
Lynn Reid Banks
Faith Ringgold
J.D. Salinger
Charles Schulz
Maurice Sendak
P.L. Travers
Garth Williams

VOLUME 3

Candy Dawson Boyd
Ray Bradbury
Gwendolyn Brooks
Ralph W. Ellison
Louise Fitzhugh
Jean Craighead George
E.L. Konigsburg
C.S. Lewis
Fredrick L. McKissack
Patricia C. McKissack
Katherine Paterson
Anne Rice
Shel Silverstein
Laura Ingalls Wilder

VOLUME 4

Betsy Byars
Chris Carter
Caroline B. Cooney
Christopher Paul Curtis
Anne Frank
Robert Heinlein
Marguerite Henry
Lois Lowry
Melissa Mathison
Bill Peet
August Wilson

VOLUME 5

Sharon Creech
Michael Crichton
Karen Cushman
Tomie dePaola
Lorraine Hansberry
Karen Hesse
Brian Jacques
Gary Soto
Richard Wright
Laurence Yep

VOLUME 6

Lloyd Alexander
Paula Danziger
Nancy Farmer
Zora Neale Hurston
Shirley Jackson
Angela Johnson
Jon Krakauer
Leo Lionni
Francine Pascal
Louis Sachar
Kevin Williamson

VOLUME 7

William H. Armstrong
Patricia Reilly Giff
Langston Hughes
Stan Lee
Julius Lester
Robert Pinsky
Todd Strasser
Jacqueline Woodson
Patricia C. Wrede
Jane Yolen

VOLUME 8

Amelia Atwater-Rhodes
Barbara Cooney
Paul Laurence Dunbar
Ursula K. Le Guin

Farley Mowat
Naomi Shihab Nye
Daniel Pinkwater
Beatrix Potter
Ann Rinaldi

VOLUME 9

Robb Armstrong
Cherie Bennett
Bruce Coville
Rosa Guy
Harper Lee
Irene Gut Opdyke
Philip Pullman
Jon Scieszka
Amy Tan
Joss Whedon

VOLUME 10

David Almond
Joan Bauer
Kate DiCamillo
Jack Gantos
Aaron McGruder
Richard Peck
Andrea Davis Pinkney
Louise Rennison
David Small
Katie Tarbox

VOLUME 11

Laurie Halse Anderson
Bryan Collier
Margaret Peterson
    Haddix
Milton Meltzer
William Sleator
Sonya Sones
Genndy Tartakovsky
Wendelin Van Draanen
Ruth White

VOLUME 12

An Na
Claude Brown
Meg Cabot
Virginia Hamilton
Chuck Jones
Robert Lipsyte
Lillian Morrison
Linda Sue Park
Pam Muñoz Ryan
Lemony Snicket
    (Daniel Handler)

VOLUME 13

Andrew Clements
Eoin Colfer
Sharon Flake
Edward Gorey
Francisco Jiménez
Astrid Lindgren
Chris Lynch
Marilyn Nelson
Tamora Pierce
Virginia Euwer Wolff

VOLUME 14

Orson Scott Card
Russell Freedman
Mary GrandPré
Dan Greenburg
Nikki Grimes
Laura Hillenbrand
Stephen Hillenburg
Norton Juster
Lurlene McDaniel
Stephanie S. Tolan

VOLUME 15

Liv Arnesen
Edward Bloor
Ann Brashares
Veronica Chambers
Mark Crilley
Paula Fox
Diana Wynne Jones
Victor Martinez
Robert McCloskey
Jerry Scott and Jim
    Borgman

VOLUME 16

Ludwig Bemelmans
Billy Collins
Tom Feelings
Tina Fey
Joy Hakim
Polly Horvath
Tim LaHaye and
    Jerry B. Jenkins
Donna Jo Napoli
Christopher Paolini
Lori Aurelia William

Business Leaders

VOLUME 1

Warren Buffett
Peter Capolino
Michael Dell
Earl Graves
Michele Hoskins
Judy McGrath
Arturo R. Moreno
Pleasant T. Rowland
Martha Stewart
Oprah Winfrey

Performing Artists

VOLUME 1

Jackie Chan
Dixie Chicks
Kirsten Dunst
Suzanne Farrell
Bernie Mac
Shakira
Isaac Stern
Julie Taymor
Usher
Christina Vidal

VOLUME 2

Ashanti
Tyra Banks
Peter Jackson
Norah Jones
Quincy Jones
Avril Lavigne
George López
Marcel Marceau
Eddie Murphy
Julia Stiles

VOLUME 3

Michelle Branch
Cameron Diaz
Missy Elliott
Evelyn Glennie
Benji Madden
Joel Madden
Mike Myers
Fred Rogers

Twyla Tharp
Tom Welling
Yuen Wo-Ping

Scientists & Inventors

VOLUME 1

John Bardeen
Sylvia Earle
Dian Fossey
Jane Goodall
Bernadine Healy
Jack Horner
Mathilde Krim
Edwin Land
Louise & Mary Leakey
Rita Levi-Montalcini
J. Robert Oppenheimer
Albert Sabin
Carl Sagan
James D. Watson

VOLUME 2

Jane Brody
Seymour Cray
Paul Erdös
Walter Gilbert
Stephen Jay Gould
Shirley Ann Jackson
Raymond Kurzweil
Shannon Lucid
Margaret Mead
Garrett Morgan
Bill Nye
Eloy Rodriguez
An Wang

VOLUME 3

Luis W. Alvarez
Hans A. Bethe
Gro Harlem Brundtland
Mary S. Calderone
Ioana Dumitriu
Temple Grandin
John Langston
    Gwaltney
Bernard Harris
Jerome Lemelson
Susan Love
Ruth Patrick
Oliver Sacks
Richie Stachowski

VOLUME 4

David Attenborough
Robert Ballard
Ben Carson
Eileen Collins
Biruté Galdikas
Lonnie Johnson
Meg Lowman
Forrest Mars Sr.
Akio Morita
Janese Swanson

VOLUME 5

Steve Case
Douglas Engelbart
Shawn Fanning
Sarah Flannery
Bill Gates
Laura Groppe
Grace Murray Hopper
Steven Jobs
Rand and Robyn Miller
Shigeru Miyamoto
Steve Wozniak

VOLUME 6

Hazel Barton
Alexa Canady
Arthur Caplan
Francis Collins
Gertrude Elion
Henry Heimlich
David Ho
Kenneth Kamler
Lucy Spelman
Lydia Villa-Komaroff

VOLUME 7

Tim Berners-Lee
France Córdova
Anthony S. Fauci
Sue Hendrickson
Steve Irwin
John Forbes Nash, Jr.
Jerri Nielsen
Ryan Patterson
Nina Vasan
Gloria WilderBrathwaite

VOLUME 8

Deborah Blum
Richard Carmona
Helene Gayle
Dave Kapell
Adriana C. Ocampo

John Romero
Jamie Rubin
Jill Tarter
Earl Warrick
Edward O. Wilson

VOLUME 9

Robert Barron
Regina Benjamin
Jim Cantore
Marion Donovan
Michael Fay
Laura L. Kiessling
Alvin Poussaint
Sandra Steingraber
Edward Teller
Peggy Whitson

Sports

VOLUME 1

Hank Aaron
Kareem Abdul-Jabbar
Hassiba Boulmerka
Susan Butcher
Beth Daniel
Chris Evert
Ken Griffey, Jr.
Florence Griffith Joyner
Grant Hill
Greg LeMond
Pelé
Uta Pippig
Cal Ripken, Jr.
Arantxa Sanchez
    Vicario
Deion Sanders
Tiger Woods

VOLUME 2

Muhammad Ali
Donovan Bailey
Gail Devers
John Elway
Brett Favre
Mia Hamm
Anfernee "Penny"
    Hardaway
Martina Hingis
Gordie Howe
Jack Nicklaus
Richard Petty
Dot Richardson
Sheryl Swoopes
Steve Yzerman

VOLUME 3

Joe Dumars
Jim Harbaugh
Dominik Hasek
Michelle Kwan
Rebecca Lobo
Greg Maddux
Fatuma Roba
Jackie Robinson
John Stockton
Picabo Street
Pat Summitt
Amy Van Dyken

VOLUME 4

Wilt Chamberlain
Brandi Chastain
Derek Jeter
Karch Kiraly
Alex Lowe
Randy Moss
Se Ri Pak
Dawn Riley
Karen Smyers
Kurt Warner
Serena Williams

VOLUME 5

Vince Carter
Lindsay Davenport
Lisa Fernandez
Fu Mingxia
Jaromir Jagr
Marion Jones
Pedro Martinez
Warren Sapp
Jenny Thompson
Karrie Webb

VOLUME 6

Jennifer Capriati
Stacy Dragila
Kevin Garnett
Eddie George
Alex Rodriguez
Joe Sakic
Annika Sorenstam
Jackie Stiles
Tiger Woods
Aliy Zirkle

VOLUME 7

Tom Brady
Tara Dakides
Alison Dunlap

Sergio Garcia
Allen Iverson
Shirley Muldowney
Ty Murray
Patrick Roy
Tasha Schwiker

VOLUME 8

Simon Ammann
Shannon Bahrke
Kelly Clark
Vonetta Flowers
Cammi Granato
Chris Klug
Jonny Moseley
Apolo Ohno
Sylke Otto
Ryne Sanborn
Jim Shea, Jr.

VOLUME 9

Tori Allen
Layne Beachley
Sue Bird
Fabiola da Silva
Randy Johnson
Jason Kidd
Tony Stewart
Michael Vick
Ted Williams
Jay Yelas

VOLUME 10

Ryan Boyle
Natalie Coughlin
Allyson Felix
Dallas Friday
Jean-Sébastien Giguère
Phil Jackson
Keyshawn Johnson
Tiffeny Milbrett
Alfonso Soriano
Diana Taurasi

VOLUME 11

Laila Ali
Josh Beckett
Cheryl Ford
Tony Gonzalez
Ellen MacArthur
Tracy McGrady
Steve McNair
Ryan Newman
Tanya Streeter
Natasha Watley

VOLUME 12

Freddy Adu
Tina Basich
Sasha Cohen
Dale Earnhardt, Jr.
LeBron James
Carly Patterson
Albert Pujols
Michael Strahan
Teresa Weatherspoon